Guys in Suits

Other books by Van Whitfield

Something's Wrong with Your Scale!

Beeperless Remote

Guys in Suits

a novel

Van Whitfield

Doubleday

New York   London   Toronto   Sydney   Auckland

PUBLISHED BY DOUBLEDAY
a division of Random House, Inc.
1540 Broadway, New York, New York 10036

DOUBLEDAY and the portrayal of an anchor with a dolphin
are trademarks of Doubleday,
a division of Random House, Inc.

Book design by Chris Welch

Library of Congress Cataloging-in-Publication Data
Whitfield, Van.
Guys in suits : a novel / Van Whitfield.—1st ed.
p. cm.
1. Triangles (Interpersonal relations)—Fiction. 2. Dating
(Social customs)—Fiction. 3. Male friendship—Fiction. I. Title.
PS3573.H4914 G89 2001
813'.54—dc21
00-065976

ISBN 0-385-49846-2

"Women don't know what they want!"
—*Simon Washington*
and Stuart A. Worthington

The 60-Day Relationship Rule For Guys

Weeks 1-2

The Glory Days

You Actually Like Her

Weeks 2-4

The Realm of Reality

The Gloss Wears Off

Weeks 5-6

The Prozac Period

She Thinks You're Mr. Right

You Know You're in Too Deep

Weeks 7-8

The Dawn of Destruction

You're Ready to Call It Quits . . .

She Isn't

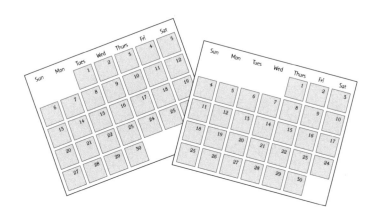

chapter 1

The Bus Driver

October 25, 2000

Simon

magine your life as a championship football game. If you pick up a yard and scamper into the end zone, that gleaming Super Bowl trophy is yours. You're going to Disney World! That picture on the Wheaties box, it's yours! And most important, besides a trip to the White House and a downtown tickertape parade, you'll get the girl. All it takes is a yard. Thirty-six measly inches. And your life will be forever changed.

But the linebacker on the other side of the ball isn't having it. He could care less about the trophy. He hates parades. And as far as he's concerned, Disney World is an overblown Florida swamp inhabited by a cartoon rat with size-nineteen feet. You and he couldn't be more different. You're playing for the whole bag of chips, but his purpose is single-minded.

He wants the girl.

The whistle blows, the fans in the packed stadium roar and, in an instant, there's a collision on the field that's so loud, it scares the guys stealing cars all the way out in the parking lot. A pile of grossly overdeveloped guys in grossly oversized pads will tell the final tale. The linebacker motions wildly and drives the crowd to a frenzy. A sack has ended the game, and you can hardly wait for the dust to clear. You're anxious because you know it's over. And because at the bottom of that pile is a man gasping for air and hoping that John Madden and the folks at Fox have cut to commercial.

The guy at the bottom is you.

You never made the Wheaties box. The invite to Disney World must have gotten lost in the mail. And you absolutely didn't get the girl. She was too busy posing with the linebacker at what was supposed to be *your* parade.

I can relate to your dilemma. I feel your pain. Because like you, I've been sacked.

That's my life.

We were knee-deep into a new millennium and I had nothing to show for it. No wife. No girlfriend. I didn't even have the ever-present "girl you call in a pinch."

The one thing I did have was a job. I was a mass transit

operator. You'd probably have called me a bus driver. And I probably wouldn't have answered. I didn't drive a bus. I operated a vehicle. I didn't grow up thinking I'd one day be a major cog in the nation's capitol's mass transit system, but over the years, my career choice had grown on me. I was proud of what I did and I was good at it. Sometimes career choices fall into your lap. That's how it worked for me.

Literally.

It happened eight years ago on the F-14 route, which connects D.C. to the Maryland suburb I called home, Capitol Heights. I was a slim and trim twenty-one-year-old stud and had just finished a game with my flag football team. My teammates all had cars or rides with their girlfriends to ensure their ways home. All I had was a beat-up pair of cleats and a bus token.

Thankfully, I located a stop about a block from the field, and when a vehicle pulled up, I wearily climbed on board and made my way toward the dreaded "back of the bus." I was dead tired and reasoned that sitting away from the other passengers would afford me a bit of privacy and a well-deserved nap. As we rolled down Benning Road and slowly crept past one of D.C.'s old-school culinary landmarks, the Shrimp Boat, I had no idea my life would soon change in ways I never imagined.

I was on my way to the Super Bowl!

When we stopped at Texas Avenue, a woman stepped aboard, and I immediately felt I was in the throes of a medical calamity. She was so thoroughly beautiful that I first thought I was paralyzed. Seconds later, my heart was racing so fast I could have sworn I was having a heart attack. And immediately thereafter, I worried I'd been struck with lockjaw, because I literally felt I couldn't speak. A fact that was plainly evident when she smiled at me and asked, "Is that seat taken?"

"S-s-seat?" I nervously stuttered.

"The blue one beside you," she replied, still standing. "I assume it's available."

"The seat?" I repeated.

"Yes," she answered, starting to sit. "I know I didn't have to ask, but I figured, 'he looks pretty tired,' so I went with it."

"Yeah," I said, sitting up from my slouch. "I'm pooped."

"So you're a football player," she observed.

"The jersey gives it away, huh?" I replied.

"Actually, it's the cleats," she acknowledged, looking down. "Anybody can sport a jersey," she added. "But you don't run into too many people wearing cleats."

"Point well taken."

"Did you win?"

"Win what?" I asked.

"Your game," she asked, suddenly turning toward me.

"Don't take this wrong," I quickly answered. "But do I know you?" I asked, noticing that she seemed far too friendly to be a D.C. gal.

"Not yet," she admitted, reaching for my hand. "But if you play your cards right, who knows?"

"Do you realize your hand is on top of mine?" I asked, surprised.

"Are you saying you don't like it when the woman's on top?"

"That depends on what she's doing when she's on top," I told her.

"Just go along with me here," she whispered, smiling. "One of my customers just got on and if he sees me in public, I want him to see me with somebody."

"Somebody?" I asked, concerned.

"If he sees me with you, maybe he'll think I'm taken and I can get him off my back," she remarked. "You know how you men are," she went on, still forcing a smile. "He bought me a drink and then he acted like I was his personal property."

"What do you do?" I asked, trying to spot her "customer." "Are you a hair stylist or something?"

"Not quite," she answered, reaching into a soft leather handbag. "But if you go get yourself cleaned up you can come down and see me," she said, handing me a glossy red note card.

"Get it at Vic's," I read from the card. "What do you get?"

"Maybe you'll get me," she answered, starting to stand. "It's right over there," she said, pointing. "Hopefully, you'll make it through."

She then smiled, blew me a kiss and winked before stepping away from the vehicle.

She didn't need to worry about me getting there. I'd miss club-level luxury box seats to the NFL Hall of Fame game first. It took me all of thirty minutes to shower, dress and make my way back into town, where I quickly learned that among the craziest places in D.C., Vic's was perhaps the craziest.

I should have expected no less. Especially from a business that billed itself as equal parts barbecue pit and lowdown "get your money's worth" strip lounge.

The moment I walked in, I couldn't help but notice that

the walls were painted in the blackest of black. Four well-placed neon signs flashed Get It At Vic's almost in unison. A nonstop showcase of strobe lights, beacons and wannabe lasers gave the main hall a peculiar glow. The bar was shiny and very long. It was stocked with everything from mind-numbing malt liquors like Olde English and St. Ides to smooth and sassy fine liqueurs like Canadian Mist and Courvoisier.

At Vic's, the music came in one easily distinguishable form—loud—and the main hall carried the airy aroma of fresh barbecue. It always struck me as odd that guys would actually want to suck on a rib bone while stuffing a five-spot down some dancer's overworked G-string, but Vic had it all figured out. He knew that guys could deal with the hickory redolence of ribs and rib juice over the crotch-grinding bouquet of a dozen sweat-glazed, naked strippers and their juices any day of the week.

Vic's was known to have the best strippers in the city. The clubs in the upscale northwest section of the city had ladies who didn't really want to strip. They preferred to dance and wiggle. In Northeast D.C. the strippers were hard-core. Which would work, except that they looked hard-core. In Southeast, where Vic's was located, strippers stripped. And Vic's had the best of them. Vic's girls didn't seem to have a problem with what they did. In fact, it almost seemed like they enjoyed it.

Especially the woman I'd met on the bus. She spotted me, smiled and headed toward my table.

"You made it," she said, sounding almost happy.

"So this is what you do?" I asked.

"It's just a way to make a buck," she insisted. "Don't let it faze you," she added, now seated in my lap.

"How can it *not* faze me when you're doing that?" I asked, referring to her grinding in my crotch.

"I thought you didn't like the woman on top," she said, giggling.

"Since you're on top," I said, trying to maintain composure, "I guess introductions are in order. I'm Simon," I told her. "What's your name?"

"What's your favorite candy bar?"

"Snickers."

"Try again," she insisted.

"PayDay?" I asked, still trying to hold it together.

"Think of something sweet and chocolatey," she whispered.

"I don't know," I replied, my hand crawling up her thigh. "What's candy got to do with it?"

"You think I'm sweet, don't you?" she asked, sounding innocent.

"Right about now I think you're anything you want to be," I reasoned.

"Good," she said, firmly grabbing my hand. "Use this to get your wallet—and call me Kit Kat."

Kit Kat.

When her shift was done, she gave back the money and told me she liked me. We later ended up at my place and, within an hour, my virginity was history. I'd like to believe I lost my virginity three times that night, but I'm told losing it only counts for the "official" first time. Kit, as she liked to be called, changed my life almost overnight. I went from being a geeky post-teenager with a dead-end part-time job to a responsible guy with a career and future I appreciated. She was the one who convinced me to apply with Metro. "My best customers are bus drivers," she told me. "And they're never short for cash. You'll do good with it and to tell the truth, I can't resist a man in uniform."

That's all I needed to hear. I hated suits. She liked blue collar guys. And I'd have all the tip money I could handle. Was there anything not to like?

Kit and I learned the city together. We would joke and laugh long into the night and make love past sunrise. She came to be many things to me. I saw her as a friend and a trusted confidante who was bright beyond belief. She knew how much I loved football and came to all my games and was my biggest, if not only, fan. But her most endearing quality was the very same one that frustrated me most. She was as mysterious as a "Twilight Zone" episode.

I never knew where she lived and never learned a thing about her family. I didn't even know her real name. She guarded her privacy better than the U.S. Mint guards gold in Fort Knox, and she maintained control like an NFL head coach during the dog days of summer training camp. We dated for a solid year and at her best she was an un-nerving set of contradictions. I came to simultaneously see her as the everyday girl next door *and* the alluring lady who had to be from out of town. She was the girl you couldn't wait to take home *and* the woman you wouldn't dare take near your family. She could stir the very core of your imagination and was as unpredictable as a mid-August Gulf Coast hurricane.

And much like a tiny island that's hit when a hurricane strikes, when she was done with me, I was devastated. Inside a year, my life had evolved. I had dignity and purpose and had learned the joys of commitment. And then one day out of nowhere, she dropped me. She sent a note that simply read: "Simon—It's over."

And that was that. No explanation. No long drawn-out speeches. Just typical Kit, straight and to the point: "It's over." I still had that note. It haunted me from the bottom of my dresser drawer. It's as if it spoke out and reminded me that I never once told Kit how I felt about her, and that I had no clue as to what she saw in me. Sometimes it felt like all we did was enjoy each other's company. Dreams and goals and ambitions never found a way into our conversations. And feelings . . . they were never discussed.

Not even in the note.

And every time I met a woman and we even dared to get close, I read that note and headed myself straight for the hills. "It's over." The words cut to the core. But I was tired of being cut and after eight years of going it alone, I'd decided I wanted what every man really wants. Happiness was just around the corner and I was going to find it.

I wanted a relationship.

I was ready to get back to the Super Bowl!

And just two weeks ago, that theory was put to the test. I ran into Kit, but instead of throwing a touchdown, my pass fell short and was, sadly, incomplete. I thought I'd gotten over her. But when she stepped onto the F-14, the very same route we'd met on, the pounding in my heart and the haze in my head convinced me I hadn't.

The F-14 had grown to be my favorite route because it was full of women. Inner-city single moms with good jobs, good money and sturdy, serviceable bodies made it the route to run. Meeting chicks was a breeze on the F-14. If you had half a rap, you were in the house. My rap might have been weak, but they knew I was employed, which meant I had benefits. They couldn't get to work, to the bank, to day-care or to the liquor store to play their numbers without me. They knew it. I knew it. And if I even remotely felt that women had a clue as to what they wanted in a man, I'd use those facts to my advantage like a nappy-headed teenager uses extensions.

Kit didn't recognize me at first. She dropped her dollar and carefully reached over to pick it up.

"That's a switch," I said, laughing.

"Excuse me?" she said, adjusting her sleek wire-frame glasses.

"That's a switch," I repeated, still laughing. "You never used to drop dollar bills, you were always picking them up."

She looked at me, puzzled.

"Simon?" she asked, stunned. "I hardly recognized you. You've put on weight," she observed. "Are you still playing football?"

"Eight years of good eating will do that to you," I acknowledged. "And I haven't picked up the pigskin in years."

She parked herself on the handicap seat right behind me. Kit still looked good. Her skin appeared to be as soft and smooth as a Boyz II Men ballad. Her full, pouting lips eased into an inviting smile when she eased out of shock and finally recognized me. Her perfectly centered nose gave way to a set of perfect almond-shaped eyes, deep brown in color, sweet and seductive. She was blessed with the most alluring eyes I'd ever seen. Her auburn-streaked shoulder-length hair was curled into a cute well-kept style. Sassy and playful. Just like I remembered her. Kit was still a bronze goddess with a devil of a body.

The conversation was actually awkward. Think about it. Where did you pick up with a woman who broke your heart and walked away smiling?

"So what you been up to?" I asked, self-consciously checking my rearview mirror.

"I'm a broker."

"You're a broker?"

"Yes, Simon," she answered. "I am a broker."

"How did someone like you end up being a broker?" I asked.

"I don't know what you mean by 'someone like me,' Simon," she said. "I wasn't 'someone like me' when we dated," she went on. "I was once a dancer," she continued. "And you were once an easy mark," she added coldly. "I would like to think we're both beyond that."

The conversation wasn't going exactly like I hoped. I checked both my rearview and cabin mirrors as we pulled away from the next stop. I was thinking of how I could work her toward a date.

"Are you beyond that, Simon?" she said, her voice rising. "Do you still hang out at Vic's?"

A hush fell over the vehicle. I couldn't believe that she called me out like that. I just knew that all eyes and ears were on me. A quick glance in my cabin mirror verified my worst thoughts. They all stared at me while leaning

forward in their seats. There was no doubt they were waiting for an answer. I wasn't about to give it to them. It
didn't help when one of my favorite passengers, Mrs. Mer-
riweather, broke the silence and said, "Well?" It also didn't
help when we passed Vic's. To add insult to injury, at the
very next stop, Mr. Victor D'mazio, the Vic of Vic's Strip
Lounge and Barbecue Pit, boarded the vehicle.

Victor D'mazio had a stirring Italian accent. He was always laughing, telling ridiculously unfunny jokes and
smiling like he'd just bought a time-share at Happiness
Estates. If you didn't know him, you would have thought
he was the king of the world, instead of the king of D.C.'s
strip joints.

Vic dressed like he was just a call away from being cast
as the lead in *Godfather* XXV. Tailored Italian sharkskin
suits, bold Versace ties with diamond-studded tiepins,
and immaculately polished Gucci loafers were staples of
his wardrobe. Vic always wore a fresh white carnation on
his left lapel. Monogrammed onyx cuff links embraced his
wrists. Custom-made Stetson hats enveloped the healthy
flock of silver hair that covered his head. Vic was a classic.
The elder statesman of strip clubs, who talked with his
hands. He was cool. He was a stand-up guy. And he always
had a kind word.

"Simon," he said, smiling. "Where you been? We
haven't seen you in two weeks."

Kit couldn't contain herself. She laughed. Every passenger on the vehicle laughed. And Vic sat down right next to
Kit.

"How are you, sweetheart?" he asked, reaching for her
hand. "Are you taking care of my money?"

"We probably shouldn't discuss this here, but let's just say things are looking very good," she answered, smiling. "Remember that little software company I told you about?"

"Of course I remember," he answered in a huff. "I also remember telling you I didn't like all that computer stuff."

"You don't have to like it," she said, smiling. "But you own five hundred shares of their stock. And since it jumped nearly fifty dollars a share, I figure you can learn to like it."

Vic was stunned.

"Get a load of this, Simon," he said, standing up. "I tell her to take care of my money and she invests it in something I don't even like."

He then moved toward the door. Vic hopped on the F-14 every morning so he could have breakfast at Tony's Backstreet Kitchen. It was only three blocks from his spot, but Vic didn't walk anywhere. And he wasn't about to park his pet ride, a classic 1965 Rolls-Royce Silver Shadow, in front of Tony's. A Rolls wasn't exactly the type of vehicle that you put "The Club" on when you parked, so I don't blame him.

Before Vic stepped off he said, "Evelyn, you are brilliant. Come see me. I need to tell you what else I don't like." He tipped his hat, blew her a kiss with *both* hands and stepped away laughing.

I glanced at the cabin mirror to check on my passengers. You constantly had to look out on the F-14, because it was the preferred downtown route for every parolee and bail-jumper in the city. They knew that the chances of them running into a parole officer, a cop or any other law enforcement official they weren't trying to see was near zero on the F-14. I thought of what to say next to Kit. I couldn't believe she had hit it big. When it struck me that she was on the F-14, I realized she couldn't have hit it that big.

"So, Kit," I started.

"My name is Evelyn."

"Kit, Evelyn, Evelyn, Kit. What's the difference?"

"The difference is my name is Evelyn."

"Okay," I said, while turning onto Thirteenth Street. "So, Evelyn."

"Call me Eve."

"Eve, Evelyn, whatever."

"Eve," she said, sighing.

"Okay, Eve," I said. "What's a big bad broker like you doin' on the F-14? Your Honda in the shop or something?"

"No, Simon," she said, smiling. "My *Lexus* is parked at my office."

"Lexus?" I said, surprised. "You sure it's not one of those Acura Integras?"

"You are funny, Simon."

We were at Metro Center, which connected D.C. to the rest of the metropolitan area. It was also the end of the F-14. I'd nearly blown it. But there was still time to make a move. I didn't see a ring, so I gathered that she was still single. And at twenty-nine, she had the trendy style, good looks and tight body of a much younger woman. She was definitely a catch. The type who could draw me back into the game in an instant. And the Super Bowl, the trophy and the parade that I'd waited on for years would be mine.

Eve might have been a broker, but she still hung around the way. Nobody rode the F-14 unless they had to. I tried to think of something slick to say as she stood and reached for her briefcase.

"Just in case you really wanted to know," she said. "I'll be taking this route every Wednesday because I just started a breakfast mentor group for young ladies who are interested in the business world. It's my way of giving back, of keeping it real."

The slick line I was waiting for betrayed me. It was nowhere to be found. My prospects for a date were fading faster than Terrance Trent Darby's singing career. It was cool, though. I figured she probably thought she was too good for me now anyway.

She stepped off the bus and did a dainty little turn.

"Nice seeing you, Simon," she said.

She then smiled, blew me a kiss and winked just like she had when I first met her on the F-14 eight years ago.

"By the way, Simon," she said softly. "I definitely don't drive an Integra. I drive a Lexus coupe."

Damn, I thought, frustrated. Kit the dancer is now Evelyn the broker. And, ironically, she still makes money for Vic. She drives a Lexus *and not* an Integra. And I let her get away without even trying to get a date.

"And Simon," she said before leaving. "I know I told you to take this job, but I didn't think you'd *still* be a bus driver."

"I am not a bus driver!" I yelled as the passenger entry doors of my vehicle slammed together. "I am a mass transit operator!"

I stared blankly as she walked into the subway station.

She stepped onto an escalator and, with her hand at her brow, blocked away the early morning sun.

This couldn't be any worse, I thought watching her disappear out of the haze and down into the subway. *I'll never get to the Super Bowl.*

chapter 2

The Stockbroker

That Same Day

Stuart

Women are like Firestone tires. They should come with expiration dates.

Think about it.

After sixty days, they lose it. It's why intelligent, desirable men like me lived by the "60 day rule," a theory that made the rounds during my junior year at Princeton.

The first two weeks, days one to fourteen, actually work. They were known as the "Glory Days." This is a time spent in a state of semiblissful ignorance. You like each other. You actually *want* to talk. And when you scribble your names together, it brings a smile.

Weeks three and four, the "realm of reality," are different. Concern creeps in and the gloss eerily wears off. The fresh perm from week one needs, can we say, a touch-up. And when you blow bubbles with your straw in a glass of Coke, she's no longer impressed with what she thought was youthful energy during the first two weeks; now she thinks you're childish. You start to see each other as real people as opposed to the can-do-no-wrong slices of perfection you'd always dreamed of and concocted in your mind.

The fifth and sixth weeks are filled with anxiety. We called this the "Prozac Period." She's worried about your real intentions and you're worried that you're already in over your head. But the real stress is simple—you both want to hop in the sack, to see if getting to the next two weeks is worth it.

And the "Dawn of Destruction," the final two weeks, represent a time of cold, brutal reality. The huge mistake from the Prozac Period (i.e., sleeping together) comes to fruition. You both regret it and wish you could take it back. She's worried that you see her as another notch on your belt, and you're worried that she sees you as the man she's ready to settle down with. You no longer scribble the other's name in delight. You sneer and mark through it in contempt. And the sad, sad truth is that both of you want exactly the same thing.

To be back at the first two weeks.

And this is precisely where women lose it.

Instead of walking away, they believe in working things out. The guy's ready to go. He understands the 60 day rule. But she insists, "If you just communicate with me—like you did in the first week!—we can work this out." She just doesn't realize the only thing he really wants to communicate is his desire to move on, and get another 60 day lease on happiness. He knows it will never work, but he won't say a word because guys are wimps.

Thankfully, happening men like myself weren't often forced to do the wimp thing. The 60 day rule was my credo. I followed it to the letter and I was usually happy with the results. I met lots of women. Went out as often as I could. And instead of chasing women down and playing the pursuit game, I made them—check me out!

Check me out!

Those words were like gold.

I'd come upon the phrase shortly after I finished my MBA three years ago.

I was in celebration mode and was sipping on champagne in the VIP lounge at Zanzibar, the club at the waterfront. Some halfway loaded hot-body in a tight red dress walked up to me, and it was clear she was ready for action. But she had "issues." Problem one, her appearance. She was cute and her body had considerable assets, but she wasn't the "package." Had she been without the cheap turned-over shoes, the half-done, peeling nails and the knotted-root twelve-dollar perm, she'd have made any man's "potential" list. But facts are facts, so she might as well have walked in, grabbed a drink and screamed, "I drive a four-door family sedan!" Which might have been a good approach for men who dated sedan types and who had kids.

I didn't.

Problem two, her approach. It was as weak as a four-cylinder 1988 Toyota Tercel.

"If you were as cute as you *think* you are, you'd be dangerous," she told me.

"Is that right?" I remarked, carefully sizing her up. "And if I wasn't as cute as you *know* I am, your cute behind wouldn't be wasting your teeth by smiling in my face," I answered, lowering my drink. "Now stand back and watch me work."

"Watch you what?" she asked, surprised.

"Check me out," I said, slowly rubbing my hands together.

I caught a glimpse of myself in the mirror behind the bar, gave myself a well-deserved wink, patted my lapels and hit a slow, steady stride toward the dance floor. I took my time because she needed to catch every single moment of what she could have had.

I wanted her to—Check Me Out!

Unfortunately, my trip to the dance floor failed to be the picture of grace and grandeur I'd expected. I walked right into a woman who was engaged in a celebration all her own. And when her drink found a spot on my lapel, trouble was a beat away. Champagne and silk are like oil and water—they don't mix.

"Look miss," I said, reaching for a napkin. "This is rare Italian silk," I told her, wiping my jacket. "And I hope you like it," I finished. "Because you just bought it."

"It has to be rare," she answered, starting to laugh. "Exactly how many fools do you think would actually buy one of these?"

"Are you saying—"

"Did you buy it?" she interrupted.

"Well I guess that makes you a fool too," I shot back. "Because it's yours now," I added, removing my jacket and handing it to her.

"Feels nice," she remarked, opening it. "And look," she added. "It's a Stuart A. Worthington," she laughed. "Is Stuart A. Worthington the male equivalent to the Martha Stewart line at Kmart?"

"I can't say that I've ever been to Kmart," I answered.

"So where does one buy a Stuart A. Worthington?"

"One doesn't," I told her, smiling. "And besides," I said, slowly sizing her up, "I doubt you could afford me."

"That's you?" she said, glancing at my name, etched on the jacket lining. "You're a designer?"

"*I'm* a financial planner," I admitted, whipping out a business card. "And my name is in all of my jackets."

"How sweet," she replied. "And does Mommy still write your name in your underwear too?"

"Are you trying to find out?" I quickly asked.

She had to find out. She was a woman. She couldn't resist.

And as gorgeous as she was, I couldn't resist her myself. While the hot-body in the red dress stood by and checked me out, we took to the floor and danced the night away. I learned that her name was Lynn. And she was the type who had more questions than answers. She asked how long I'd been a *stockbroker* and I nearly flipped.

"I totally reject that term," I told her. "I advise well-meaning folk on how to get rich. Trading stocks is just a small part of what I do," I added. "And what is it that you do for a living, Lynn?" I asked.

"I work," she answered, smiling. "And when I'm not working, I *love* to party," she said, gracefully spinning toward me.

I also learned that despite a love of heavy bass beats and DJs who knew how to keep a groove, we shared a significant quality that has doomed many—we both had to have the last word.

"What exactly makes you think you're so cute?" she asked, while we danced.

"I put the p-l-a-y in 'player'," I told her, finishing a turn. "And when 'handsome' needed help, I gave it a hand."

"If that's the case, hand*some* still needs a hand*out*," she joked.

"And so do you, Miss Lynn," I remarked, reaching out to hand-dance. "Because that jacket you just bought is worth a cool grand."

"The only thing *cool* about that jacket is the response you'll get from women when you're wearing it."

"I didn't get a cool response from you," I answered, still grooving. "I got you on the dance floor, didn't I?"

"You're not wearing the jacket," she reminded me.

That's how our relationship went. We were both masters of one-ups-man-ship, which got us nowhere fast. Despite the fact that she was incredible in the sack, we never got off the ground. Lynn's idea of dating was meeting for drinks. That got old quick. She had no tolerance for liquor and would get tipsy after just one drink. The upside was that when she said, "I think I'm a little tipsy," we'd rush to my place and have at it. The downside was that she'd pass out when we were done. It's not like I wanted to chat when we were done. And, I definitely didn't want to cuddle.

I just couldn't get her out of my place! Which made taking phone calls from my many other prospects near impossible.

I admit to going the extra mile. I *tried* to talk to her. But that was a colossal waste of time. She had more secrets than J. Edgar Hoover when he was strong-arming the FBI. And when I swallowed my pride and tried to convince her we should "move things ahead," she wasn't having it. She wanted control more than a conquering matador parading around at a bullfight.

My biggest mistake was allowing her to obliterate the 60 day rule. We hung out for a solid six months, but it wasn't what anyone would call a relationship. When the seventh month rolled around, changes were in order. I'd become a victim of the credo that had ruled my life and nearly fooled myself into thinking that a relationship was a possibility. Lynn was nice enough and she was absolutely the type you wanted to be seen with in public, but our situation gave full credence to the 60 day rule. It was to be followed religiously.

But incredible sex has caused incredible lapses of judgment for a great many men *and* women.

Unfortunately, her judgment was more accurate than mine. And Lynn, being Lynn, was bright enough, quick enough and perhaps even devious enough to beat me to the punch. It happened on an unusually warm fall night while we were standing outside D.C.'s hottest jazz spot, the

Bohemian Caverns. We'd just finished a late dinner and she looked me dead in the eye and pronounced, "I can't do this anymore." She said we'd never had a relationship in the first place and that she didn't have the time or energy to continue with a totally sexual situation. "We both deserve more than that," she reasoned.

Who deserves more than that? I wondered.

She was right, but I hated it. I still couldn't believe that she beat me to the punch! I didn't get dropped, dumped or left in the lurch by any woman. But I didn't spend a minute worrying about it. At the very same moment she was wasting her breath saying, "I can't do this anymore," I was busy checking out the smooth-legged beauty passing by behind her.

I ran into Lynn about two weeks ago. We were at a reception for Harrison, Green and Lyons, the most powerful financial-products firm in the city. She smiled when she saw me.

"Excuse me," she said, walking toward me. "But aren't you the gentleman who put the 'hand' in handsome?"

"Three years later and you're still halfway beautiful," I answered, smiling. "How goes it?"

"How would you like it to go?" she asked, placing her drink on the table beside us.

"How would *you* like it to go?"

"I think I'm a little tipsy," she said, laughing.

"At least you still have good taste," I remarked.

We left, made our way to the parking lot and stood at my shiny, new Benz while the convertible roof rolled back.

It had been some time, and I was glad she was tipsy. But for some insane reason, I found myself wanting more.

So I asked.

"Look, Lynn," I said, leaning against the door. "Why does it have to be like this? We're attracted to each other, we seem to enjoy one another's company, I respect you and I think we can do better than this."

"Does this mean you're ready to go to your place?" she asked, smiling.

"What am I doing?" I asked, frustrated. "Talking to a wall or something?"

"Stuart," she said, pulling away from me. "You are one sexy brother. But you already know that. I've told you that many times in the past."

I just looked at her, concerned. I knew where she was taking it.

"Read my lips," she said, grinning. "I may get a little tipsy around you, and I actually like the way you make me feel. You *do* know how to get the job done," she added. "But I'm not interested, searching or even thinking about a relationship, so drop it."

That's all I needed. It was dropped.

But she wasn't about to get off as easy as she had when she'd ended it three years ago.

"You know, I'm actually glad you turned me down," I said, hopping into my car. "With a little work, you'd be a real catch," I told her. "But now that I see you in the light, I have to admit—the last three years have done a number on you."

"Maybe you're right, Stuart," she fired back. "But you know how it is when they make you a *VP*," she added.

"Time flies right by you," she remarked. "But then again, you probably can't relate," she finished. "You're still a *bro-ker*, aren't you?"

"I'm not a broker, sweetie," I insisted, turning the key. "But congrats on your promo," I said, sporting a sneaky smile. "By the way," I added, ready to speed off. "Since you're a VP and all, would you be open to a little advice?"

"Of course, Stuart," she answered sarcastically. "Little minds are only capable of a *little* advice."

"Good," I said, pushing the pedal and revving the engine.

"Okay," she sighed. "What's the advice?"

"Advice?" I asked, sounding surprised.

"Yes, Stuart," she said, glancing at her watch. "I don't have any time for your games."

"You want some advice!" I exclaimed, jamming into first gear. "Here's your advice, Miss VP!" I yelled, pulling away. "Check me out!"

I was gone in a flash but I knew my next conquest would be especially satisfying.

Check me out, I thought, smiling at myself in the rearview mirror. *That gets them every time.*

chapter 3

The Bus Driver,
the Broker
and the Association

Three Weeks Later—November 16, 2000

Simon

B rothers, my brothers, what the heck is going on?"

"Who are you supposed to be—Marvin Gaye?"

"Look fellas, let's get down to business."

"That's a bet, let's do that."

"Fine. This calls to order the November 2000 meeting of the Association. Roll call, gentlemen," Trevor started.

"Drop it, Trevor. Why in the world are we doing a roll call for four people, and all of us are sitting right here in front of each other?"

Stuart was right. But it didn't much matter. Trevor

would entertain himself with roll call if he were the only one on the roll.

"Roderick Anthony Marshall."

"I'm in the house," he answered.

"Trevor Woodrow Livingston."

"This is crap," Stuart muttered.

"You just called yourself, Trevor, now you're being *too* stupid," I agreed.

"It may very well be stupid, however, I just called my name. Therefore, I am obliged to answer. I am here or as Rod so aptly put it, I too am in the house."

"Simon Washington."

"This is real stupid, Trevor."

"So too are you, Simon. Are you here?" Trevor asked.

"Am I here? If I'm not here why the heck did you just ask me if I'm here?" I answered.

"Simon Washington?"

"Are you sick, Trevor? I'm in your fricking face!"

"Last call for Simon Washington."

"He's here, Trevor. Give it a break," Rod intervened.

"Very well. Stuart Alexander Worthington."

"I don't know who's dumber, you or your wife," Stuart replied.

"That is so unnecessary. Stuart Alexander Worthington."

"Will one of you idiots kindly tell the chief idiot that this idiot refuses to participate in his idiotic roll call?" Stuart requested.

"Last call for Stuart Alexander Worthington."

"He's here, Trevor. I'm here. You're here. And Simon and Stuart are here. I think we can start now. If it's okay with you," Rod told him.

Rod hit the nail on the head. We were all in the house. The Association. Four buddies who had it going on. We gathered once a month to ponder our futures and to further our investment portfolio. Stuart knew all that we needed to know about stocks, IPOs and dot-com start-ups. After an initial outlay of one thousand dollars each and five years of shrewd, tactical investing, we had amassed what we considered to be a small fortune.

Stuart kept us up with the trends and we let it roll. Fortunately, we had been cautious with our dividends. We'd each purchased big-ticket items like cars, oversized SUVs and spacious homes. But we generally shied away from just blowing the cash. The one luxury we allowed ourselves was an all-expenses-paid winter vacation. We kicked it off each New Year's Eve and we'd visited some of the most lavish, exotic spots on the planet. The one mandatory function of the Association was to show up and live large on our vacation. It was a deal I could live with. Like all groups, we had our problems. But we trusted each other and generally got along pretty well. We'd grown up together in beautiful downtown Capitol Heights, Maryland.

Capitol Heights was the place to be during the seventies. When Black families first realized that suburban schools afforded their kids a better shot to really grab the mythical brass ring, they moved to Capitol Heights. The hilly terrain was much like that of San Francisco. The neighborhoods were latter-day suburban retreats. Half-decent lawns. Half-decent houses. Half-decent stores. And half the drugs, violence and nonsense that had come to dominate D.C.

Though D.C. and Capitol Heights were separated by just five miles and two stop lights, it seemed like they were on two entirely different continents. As the crack-cocaine turf wars of the eighties escalated, urban flight ensued. Capitol Heights served as an apt hideaway. Over the years, our neighborhood had evolved into "the hood." Our hometown was now more D.C. than D.C. ever was. And I doubt we could manage it like we did when we were coming up.

We journeyed throughout our neighborhood as if we were a modern-day Lewis and Clark expedition team. We knew where everything and everybody was. As we made the awkward transition toward adolescence, we alternated at being each other's best friends. We played ball together, cut class together and even fought when we had to. We had each other's backs. We will long be remembered for getting so blitzed at our graduation that we took turns falling down as we walked across the stage to receive our diplomas.

We were bonded to the core. After graduation, we met behind our school and bragged about how we each would conquer the world and everything in it. We were having a ball until Trevor threw up and ruined his diploma. He still couldn't handle liquor. And in the same vein, Trevor considered himself the brains of our group. He'd literally been a straight-A student. As far as we could tell, Trevor still was the smartest human being *he* ever met. On graduation day, Trevor insisted he would one day be a doctor. He breezed through undergrad at Hampton University and after that, Harvard, Yale and Duke all offered him scholarships to medical school.

His parents, who were both MDs, freaked when he jetted overseas. Trevor's girlfriend, Leigh, couldn't get into med school in the states. He, of course, couldn't imagine being away from her. It took ten years for Leigh to finish med school. Trevor pulled off a master's in public health *and* aced med school in six. They were married a month before she graduated. Their spoiled-brat, pain-in-the-behind only-child son, Trevor Woodrow Livingston III was born six months later. He wasn't premature. Leigh just played him. Though Trevor was a truly willing participant, Leigh made certain she was pregnant *before* she graduated. That way, she'd be taken care of and could put off working.

Leigh was a living testament to the existence of God. Her paralyzing good looks were clearly heaven sent. God also saved us all by assuring that Dr. Leigh L. Livingston never got close to performing any sort of medical procedure or technique on any living soul. After little Trevor was born, she promised that she would sacrifice her career to raise her son. She also promised to continue her medical career when little Trevor left for college.

I'd always considered her promise to be a threat.

Roderick Anthony Marshall wanted to see the world. He opted for the U.S. Marine Corps. When Ronald Reagan decided to rescue a group of underachieving medical students from Grenada, Rod was on the front line. Ironically, Rod claimed that the very first person he rescued was Trevor. Trevor was supposedly surrounded by a group of angry stick-wielding refugee children. He was bound, gagged and completely covered with medical tape and gauze. Rod said he thought he had uncovered either a mummy or some sort of medical experiment gone awry. He hurried to unwrap the body, and when he found it was Trevor, they both passed out.

A year later, Rod left the marines and married his high school sweetheart, Grace. He started a travel agency and Grace hit him with breathtaking twin daughters, Kokeisha and Lokeisha. They came to be known as the Koko-Loko twins. Despite the fact that his little sweethearts were also the major heartthrobs of numerous testosterone-laden teenaged boys throughout the area, Rod had maintained a happy and balanced home life. His travel agency allowed him to see the world in ways the marines never imagined. And Grace was a rock. She was smart, supportive and thoroughly independent. Rod said she was still a good lay, which wasn't really too surprising. She was the only woman he'd been with in his life, so he didn't know any better.

Stuart Alexander Worthington was my main man. He was a classic, high-strung stockbroker. The lure of easy money and the sheer greed of his many clients had propelled him toward the partner level at the stuffed-shirt brokerage house of Horton, Barber and Butler, where he worked. Stuart had all the tools—a totally awesome minimansion/bachelor pad in the superexclusive gated community of Woodmore, several slick rides, and an overblown designer wardrobe that women loved. He was smart, bold, aggressive and uncompromising, but he had one pretty significant problem. He was a total, certifiable head case. Stuart was my buddy, but he was thoroughly screwed-up. He got all the women he could handle, but he never let them stick around. Like me, he believed women didn't know what they wanted. But he took it to an extreme and insisted on always having the upper hand. Stuart was everybody's money man. He knew more about how to get cash and how to keep it than a junkie knows about getting dope and getting high.

His grandmother raised him. God broke the mold with Grandma Worthington. She firmly believed that she was ageless. Needless to say, she dressed, partied and played the role of a horny, middle-aged heiress. Being around Grandma Worthington was more like hangin' with First Cousin Worthington. Although she got around more than Stuart ever did, she kept him straight and clear of the law. Thanks to her, he was always wise to the system and how to beat it. She smoked Newports, downed white Zinfandel by the gallon and strutted to church in designer outfits by Vivienne Westwood and Karl Lagerfeld. Through Grandma Worthington, Stuart learned that just living large was not nearly enough. She lived *very* large. And also through her, he learned how to make money work.

Grandma Worthington left this earth happy. She passed while wearing a Tahari black leather miniskirt outfit. Stuart's seventy-two-year-old grandmother died while doing the macarena during a cabaret at the Panorama Room in Southeast D.C. Her thirty-six-year-old boyfriend, Rodney, tried to give her CPR. But, he didn't have much luck. Rodney insisted that she slipped him the tongue, squeezed his behind and reached for his crotch while he was trying to breathe life back into her body. He also said that her hair, makeup, lipstick and press-on nails were perfect when she passed.

None of this surprised Stuart, who was then a freshman at Princeton. He parlayed her death into a scholarship for children whose parents or guardians met their end while engaged in the performing arts. Stuart wisely invested the insurance money and the rest was history. He now played women like he played the stock market. And at twenty-nine, Stuart was still a club rat (I was certain Grandma Worthington had something to do with that). He used to talk about a woman named Lynn all the time. But I was sure she was a victim of his 60 day rule. I just hoped he still had her number. We needed dates for our annual vacation and it was only a month and a half away.

O kay gentlemen, now that we've finally finished roll call, I think we can proceed," Trevor told us.

"You can proceed to kiss my behind," Stuart huffed.

"Chill on that, Stu," Rod said, shaking his head.

"Trevor needs to chill on that," Stuart answered, obviously annoyed.

"It's a done deal, Stu," Rod insisted. "Let it go."

This was how our meetings always started. Trevor figured out a way to piss Stuart off. Stuart fell for it. And Rod refereed.

"Whatever," Stuart said, slumping into his chair.

"Fellas, as you know, our winter vacation is just around the corner. Rod, would you fill us in on this year's details?"

"You got it. Look here, this year we're gonna hit Cancun."

"Cancun?" Stuart asked, surprised.

"Yeah, Stu," Rod answered, tilting his head. "You got a problem with Cancun?"

"I thought the plan was for Hawaii."

"We *were* going to Honolulu," Trevor lectured, "but if you recall, we all agreed it was high time for us to invest some of our earnings back into the community. And the costs for Hawaii would have made that impossible."

"They don't have hula girls in Mexico!" Stuart snapped.

"Is that your only problem with Cancun, Stu?" Rod asked.

"No," he answered. "You can't drink the water in Mexico," he insisted. "And if you can't drink the water, do you really think it's okay to take a shower there?"

"You are indeed one sad brother," Trevor said, shaking his head.

"Yeah," Stuart said, sitting up in his chair, "I am one sad brother." He smiled and leaned forward. "And that wife of yours is one sad doctor."

We all laughed. This was typical Stuart-Trevor behavior. They'd done battle. Trevor always won the first round. Stuart always attacked Leigh. And the meeting always moved on.

"Simon," Rod said, still laughing. "Is Cancun okay with you?"

"I'm with it," I said, looking toward Stuart.

"I guess you would be with it," Stuart said, smiling. "You'd be with anything that got you out of your little bus."

"I don't drive a bus, Stuart," I snapped.

"Yeah," he said, laughing, "and the Pope doesn't pray to Jesus."

"Neither did your grandmother," said Trevor, smiling.

This drew an even bigger laugh than Stuart's line about Leigh.

"Cut it, Trevor," Rod said, laughing.

"It's cut."

"Look, fellas," Rod said, between laughs. "We're going to Cancun. Everything's set. We'll get there before New Year's Eve. We've got a private villa. We're having a private party. And, it is going to be top-notch."

"Sounds good to me," I said, leaning back in my chair.

"It's a plan," Trevor added.

"Whatever," said Stuart, shaking his head.

"Good," Rod stated, cleaning his glasses.

Stuart and I looked toward each other uneasily. We knew what was next.

"Gentlemen," Trevor said, deliberately. "We cannot repeat the debacle of 1999."

He's not kidding, I thought, embarrassed.

Last year we went to Monaco. Trevor and Rod had it easy. They took their wives. While Trevor sometimes came off as the truly pompous doctor that he was, Leigh was actually pretty decent. She was such a ditz that she was funny. But when she put on a bikini, she could have convinced you that her IQ was five thousand. Rod's wife, Grace, on the other hand, was perfect. Easygoing, pleasant, accommodating and self-assured. Rod had been blessed with a wife who was as regular as iced tea in August.

Stuart and I always took dates. Which underscored the fact that we were pushing thirty without wives or real relationships. It was okay though, because the dates usually worked out.

Last year they didn't.

When it looked like we were going to totally screw up and not even produce dates, we jumped on the Internet. We wandered in and out of chat rooms in a mad attempt to find two sisters or a set of friends who would take us up on our offer. A free trip to sunny Monaco. Stuart knew so many women and was so connected he could have hooked both of us up. But he thought we needed women we could "dispose of" when the trip was done. "We need somebody who won't be trying to hang around for next year's trip," he reasoned.

In a way, Stuart made sense. If you took a woman on an all-expenses-paid trip to a fancy island retreat, she'd expect and accept nothing less in the future. Instead of shopping at Target, you'd have to take her to Bloomingdale's. And McDonald's wouldn't work when some *bistro* that served cappuccino was around the corner.

We were so desperate to find women who would "lose our numbers" after the trip, that we considered offering a cash stipend for gambling. But it never got to that because, on Christmas Eve, we hit the jackpot.

Or so we thought.

Two women from Arkansas, Amber and Sonya, e-mailed us. We set up a chat session for Christmas evening. They were perfect. Twenty-six years old, fun, willing and according to them, *very able*. Fairly new boyfriends had just dumped them both so we agreed their baggage content was sufficiently low.

We figured they got hit with the classic Christmas breakup move. It saves the man from shopping or buying gifts. If he's a smart guy, he calls the day *after* Christmas. He goes on about how miserable he was without her, and says she could at least accept his gift. She falls for it. He then hits the day-after-Christmas sales which makes him look like he's the man. And he is the man. He shows up with a gift. Gets the lady back. And does it with a 50 percent savings.

We just hoped that wasn't going to be the case for Amber and Sonya. Thankfully, it wasn't. They had really been dumped. Nobody was trying to get back with anybody. We spilled the beans about Monaco and they were down. They sent us pictures, letters, bios and a huge fruit basket two days after Christmas. Rod sent them plane tickets and an itinerary. We were set.

The moment we landed in Monaco, we bought roses at the airport and waited for their flight to arrive an hour after ours. Trevor, Leigh, Rod and Grace went ahead to unpack and scope out our villa. Stuart and I both smiled as we discussed how we'd pulled off a major coup. Two fine Southern belles who were just waiting to be had. Their pictures were incredible. Leigh was fine, but Amber and Sonya's photos made her look like Whoopi Goldberg. They said all the right things in their e-mails, were always at home when we called and we had exciting four-way cybersex in private chat rooms for four nights in a row. Our time had arrived. We high-fived each other as their plane landed and happiness and good times were all we could imagine. As Stuart put it, we were ready to get paid, sprayed, made and laid.

Then they showed up.

They recognized us from our pictures. "Hey, Stuart, hey, Simon!" they yelled across the airport.

I stood frozen. Stuart had better reflexes. He ran.

"Hey, Simon," they said, approaching me. "Where did Stuart go to?"

"Huh?" I mumbled, stunned.

"Where did Stuart go to?" said the shorter woman, plastering her lips with orange lipstick. "Did he go get the limo?"

"I-I-I don't know," I said, edging backward. "I-I-I-I'll go find out."

I took off and ran right into a trash can. I didn't care that it emptied all over the freshly waxed floor, I was getting out of there. Unfortunately, Rod's travel agency was far too good. They knew exactly where we were and who to call to get to us. As Stuart and I roamed the streets of Monaco trying to figure out what to do, Amber and Sonya made their way to the villa and set up shop.

Our two gorgeous, shapely Southern belles played *us*. Amber was as short and as wide as Sonya was tall and rail-thin. They both had badly bleached blond hair with thin black roots. It was obvious their weaves could have stood a little more attention. A gold tooth encrusted with a star accented Amber's ample smile. Sonya opted for a heart. The convincing tattoos that dominated their right arms were passable self-portraits. Amber had a rottweiler, Sonya a pit bull.

Trevor and Rod didn't let up on us for the entire vacation. Leigh and Grace tried to befriend them, but that was a complete waste of time. Sonya and Amber had one agenda: food. We once ordered watermelon, and when the waiter showed up with a plate of red, ripe, freshly sliced melon, Amber said, "We asked for *a* watermelon, honey. Don't y'all git English over here?"

Our villa came stocked with food, snacks, wine and straight booze. They cleaned it out by the second day. By the fourth day, Rod told us we were reaching into next year's account. By the last day, Rod said we had exhausted next year's account, and that we wouldn't even be able to afford a vacation in our hometown of Capitol Heights.

T he final insult was a day at a topless beach. Sonya and Amber insisted that we rub sunscreen onto their woeful bodies.

Would you like us to use a dump truck? I imagined asking Amber.

I looked up, and Stuart had taken off down the beach. He spent his entire vacation running from Amber. I just shook my head, searched for a *box* of latex gloves and realized I was out of luck. It was our last day and it was almost over. I was screwed. I used the first bottle on her back. The second bottle didn't make it past her right leg and the third cried out as I spread it across her left leg. She turned over and her breasts slid to her side like two beached whales. Amber then smiled and said, "Don't stop now, honey, go head on and rub a sista down."

Sonya chimed in, "You need to move with the quickness 'cause I'm ain't waitin' long. I'm tryin' to get my tan on."

I couldn't take it. My options were limited. Plus, I was out of sunscreen.

I ran.

Stuart and I had heard about that trip every single day of every single week for almost a year. Trevor and Rod teased us. Leigh and Grace reminded us. And thanks to the magic of home video, Little Trevor and Kokeisha and Lokeisha let us have it too.

Trevor had come correct. There was no way we could afford a repeat of last year's fiasco.

"Gentlemen," Trevor said, solemnly. "Do you have dates for this year's vacation?"

"Heck yeah," Stuart answered.

"Who?!" yelled Trevor and Rod in unison.

"You don't know her."

"Do *you* know her?" they asked.

"Of course I know her," he said, squirming in his chair.

"Who is she, Stu?" Rod forcefully asked. "Is she one of your little sixty-day babes?"

"Have you actually met her?" asked Trevor.

"Look, fellas," Stuart started, "I'm going out with her as soon as you let me out of here."

Who is he talking about? I wondered.

"I'm taking Lynn," he said proudly.

"You're taking her?" I whispered, surprised.

He put his forefinger to his lips and slowly nodded as Rod and Trevor shook their heads at each other.

"What about you, Simon?" Rod said, turning toward me. "Are you going to surf the Net to find a date?"

"Or are you going to show up with somebody from your bus?" asked Trevor.

"I don't drive a bus, Trevor," I answered, frustrated.

"I don't really care what you drive, Simon," Rod said, smiling. "Just don't drive those Purina pet-food models that you drove into our vacation last year."

As always, Rod came to the rescue. Whenever we got too serious or too down on anyone, Rod broke the ice. Like a true marine, he saved me. He also bought me time. Unlike Stuart, I hadn't had a date in two months and they knew it. They weren't about to let me BS them like he had.

"I'm almost there, gentlemen," I said, lying. "I've got a date tonight too, so we need to wrap this up."

"You've got a date?" Stuart whispered, as Rod and Trevor again shook their heads at each other.

"Yeah," I whispered back. "I've got a date like you've got a date."

He nodded, smiled and gave me a well-deserved thumbs-up.

"Who might you be considering?" asked Trevor.

"I'm leaning toward this woman I used to date."

"A woman you *used* to date?" asked Rod.

"Yeah," I said, sitting forward. "I'm hooking up with Eve."

"You never mentioned an Eve," Trevor said, concerned.

"I mentioned her all right," I said, smiling. "You remember Kit Kat from Vic's?"

"Simon, we've heard about Kit Kat from Vic's, but I can't say that we've had the pleasure of meeting your little dancer friend," Trevor stated.

"I don't know if we want a dancer on our vacation who's not working as a dancer," Rod said, laughing.

"Relax," I said. "She gave that up. She's like Stuart. She's a broker now."

"Can that broker crap, Simon," Stuart said quickly. "You know I'm not a broker."

"Whatever, clown," I said, laughing.

"Yeah, Simon," Rod interrupted. "He's not a broker and you're not a bus driver."

Trevor cracked up.

"I guess you can relate, can't you, Trevor?" Stuart said.

"What do you mean, I can relate?" he answered.

"You know what I mean," Stuart said, laughing. "I'm not a broker, Simon's not a bus driver and your wife definitely isn't anybody's doctor!"

That was too funny. But the irony was that he was right. I wasn't a bus driver.

"Look, gentlemen," Trevor said, standing over us. "We all know that neither of you have dates tonight."

He was right and he knew it. We laughed.

"You guys cannot pull the same crap that you pulled last year," he said, sitting down. "We deserve better, our wives deserve better and quite frankly, you deserve better."

"Yeah, fellas," Rod said, smiling. "Cancun is like that. You don't need to waste your vacation like you did last year. I can't understand why you fools can't get wives anyway."

"First of all, I'm not interested in a wife," Stuart

started. "I don't even want a girlfriend if I have to deal with her for more than sixty days," he added. "Women don't know what they want anyway, so what's the big deal?" he asked, shaking his head.

"Yeah," I added. "We know what we want, but 2000 is almost history and believe me, it's not as easy as it was when you guys met your wives."

"Women don't know what they want!" Stuart and I chimed, together.

"They don't want any scrubs," Rod joked.

"What, pray tell, is a scrub?" Trevor asked, sounding worried.

"It's a surgical garment, fool," Stuart said, starting to laugh. "The kind your dopey wife will never wear because she's not about to operate on anybody."

We all laughed right along with him—even Trevor!

"Dig it, Rod," I said. "Women may not want a scrub. It's easy to drone on about what you don't want. But when do they ever talk about what they *do* want?"

"You have a point, Simon," Trevor added, nodding his head.

"Well, we know they don't want a short-short man," Rod joked.

"And they definitely don't appear to desire a gentleman who won't call for seven whole days," Trevor said, smiling.

"They don't want a guy who has a buddy named Tyrone." Stuart laughed.

"Who is Tyrone?" Trevor asked, concerned.

"He's the guy you'd have to call if Leigh booted you out," I told him.

"Tyrone?" Trevor repeated.

"You betta call Tyr-o-n-e," Rod and I crooned, à la Erykah Badu.

"Tyrone?" Trevor huffed. "That's so ethnic," he added. "I'm sure his last name is Jackson or something like that."

"It doesn't matter what his last name is because you wouldn't know how to call him if you had to," Stuart said, looking toward Trevor.

"That's enough, Stu," Rod interrupted. "This has nothing to do with Trevor, Leigh or anybody's Tyrone," he said. "When it comes to finding and keeping women, the cheese has slipped from your crackers."

"That it has," Trevor added, wiping his glasses. "Stuart, your sixty-day principle regarding women is *beyond* juvenile," he commented. "And Simon, the moment you realize that there's more to life than football and a trip to the Super Bowl, you'll meet someone like that," he added, snapping his fingers. "You two can blame it on women all you want, but your inability to successfully court potential paramours baffles me," he finished.

It baffled us too.

But we'd had the "women don't know what they want" talk many times over and Trevor and Rod didn't buy it because they had wives. The meeting broke up without much more fanfare. Stuart and I once again lied about having dates, and Trevor reminded us that he knew we didn't. Stuart pulled off in his Benz and I hurried home in my Range Rover. I called him when I settled in.

"What's up, Stu?" I asked.

"Hey, Simon," he answered. "We have to do something quick."

"I'm on mine," I said, flipping through my phone book for Eve's number.

"I am too," he said, turning pages in his phone book.

"Look, man," I said, as I located her number, "You can probably help me with Eve. You can tell me some of that broker crap to talk to her."

"I don't keep up with broker crap," he said, laughing. "But I'll put you down with some smooth financial lines."

"That's a bet."

"And you can help me with Lynn," he said. "Nobody knows the city like you. That crazy bus takes you everywhere."

"I don't know anything about that bus nonsense," I answered. "But you know I'll hook you up with some of my spots."

"Out," we said before hanging up.

We were on. If I played my hand right, I knew I could book Eve for the trip. I just had to make me a plan and work it. And I bet Stuart could make things work with Lynn if he got her to the right spots and decided to let her get past his sixty-day limit.

Rod was right. Cancun would be like that. I'd sport Eve. Stuart would sport Lynn. And we could finally put last year's drama to rest.

The 60-Day Rule

Weeks 1-2

The Glory Days

God I love this stage of a relationship! Early on, I like the woman, she actually *thinks* she likes me, and if only for a minute, a real bond feels possible. That's how it felt when I first met Eve, who was Kit Kat back then. I don't know that I've experienced anything more magical in my life. It was like David Blaine, the wiry illusionist who trapped himself in a huge block of ice on New York's Times Square. I couldn't believe he pulled it off anymore than I could accept that Kit Kat was actually with me around the clock. She was sunshine, candy, and Christmas all wrapped up in one. Our Glory Days were *beyond* perfect. In fact, if I could have bunched those first two weeks into one incredibly long two-week period—one that lasted say, a year—I bet we'd be married right now.

Simon Washington
The Single Bus Driver

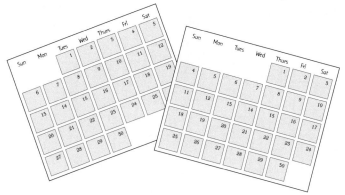

Simon, Eve, a Dance and a Cup?

Later That Night

Simon

Though I know she didn't mean to, Eve had bitten me with the relationship bug when I'd seen her two weeks earlier. I didn't just want to get her on the trip, I wanted to see if we could take a shot at making things work. But how did you approach a woman who'd been out of your life for eight years? I was willing to leave our past behind if it meant we could discuss a real future. But I had got to get my foot in the door.

There was only one way to go. I would have to use the cool approach.

"Hey, Eve, what it be?... What it look like?... What the dilly?"

Or, was it "*What's* the dilly?"

That was the problem with cool. Cool seemed like it changed every day. I couldn't believe men would waste a second worrying about the "dilly" and how to lay it out. I guarantee some mixed-up guy (one just like me) was parked in his Stratolounger worried to death about the proper use of "dilly" as it related to looking cool, in conjunction, of course, with scoring points with some woman.

The dilly?

I was worried about the dag-on "dilly" and I didn't have a clue as to what the "dilly" was in the first place.

This was why being a guy was so hard these days. And things like phones didn't help because the one I was using was already on the third ring and I didn't know what I was going to say if she answered. I only knew it had to be right and that it had to be cool. R-e-a-l cool.

"Hello," said the woman on the other end of the line.

"What the dilly?" I asked, trying to jam the words back into my mouth.

"What's the what?" she asked, alarmed.

"What the dilly?" I repeated, awkwardly.

"Is this an obscene phone call?" she inquired. "Because if it is, I have caller ID."

"We don't need to go through all that," I told her. "It's me," I said, trying to relax. "Simon Washington."

"Simon?" she said, surprised. "Why are you calling me and what is this 'what's the dilly?' thing you're talking about?"

"It's '*what* the dilly?' " I replied. "And it's just a line," I told her. "It's kind of like an icebreaker."

"It's more like an ice-*maker*," she said, with an edge. "Why in the world would a woman respond to a line as stupid as that?" she went on. "Who do you expect to pick up with something as stupid as 'what's the dilly?' and what the heck is a 'dilly' anyway?" she asked.

"I already told you it's *what* the dilly?" I reminded her. "And it's just a line, Kit, so ease up."

"Don't call me Kit, Simon. Don't go there."

"My bad."

"Why are you calling me, Simon?" she asked, sounding annoyed. "What do you want?"

"The dilly!" I said, proudly.

Click.

Click? I thought worried. I knew she hadn't hung up on me. The last woman who'd hung up on me was Sarah Jenkins. I'd asked her how she felt about three-ways and she'd freaked out.

"That's what's wrong with men!" she yelled. "I let my hair down, tell you I'm into you and you have the audacity to ask me about a three-way?" she added. "You could have at least waited until we'd done it by ourselves!"

"What the heck are you talking about, Sarah?" I asked, concerned. "I just got a call from some guy trying to convince me to upgrade my phone service and I wanted to know how you felt about three-way calling," I told her.

And then she did it.

Click.

Just like Eve.

I never called Sarah back, but I wasn't about to let this go with Eve without straightening her out. Nobody hung up on me. I didn't roll like that. It was a respect thing and she wasn't about to disrespect me without getting a piece of my mind. I hit the redial button and it was on. The moment she answered the phone, I lit in.

"No, you didn't hang up on me!" I exclaimed.

"I most certainly did," she reminded me.

"I don't think so," I said forcefully.

"Simon," she casually remarked.

"Yeah?"

Click.

Whoa, I thought, stunned. Girlfriend had hit with a big-time two-piece suit. She hung up on me like I was a doorman at Chump Towers. *What do I do here?* I wondered, worried. *If I call back, I'm a jerk. She clicked me twice. I should get the message. But if I don't call back and set her straight, I'm a prime-time candidate for Wimp of the Week.*

When a guy was screwed either way, there was only one way to go.

And my redial button was going to get me there.

"Yes, Simon," she answered.

"You're not going to hang up?" I asked, solidifying a sure Wimp of the Week nomination.

"If you can remember my name and keep your juvenile lines to yourself that's a distinct possibility," she casually stated.

"I can manage that," I told her.

"You would want to," she answered.

"Eve," I said, reaching for the remote to my living-room wide-screen. "I was just wondering what you were up to these days."

"Why in the world would you wonder about me?" she asked.

"I was just thinking we could hang out or something like that."

"And why would I want to hang out with you, Simon?"

"Because," I started. "It's Thursday night and you're sitting at home just like me."

"And?" she interrupted.

"And I figure your social life may need some attention just like mine, and since I'm slightly available, I was thinking we could hang out."

"Don't fool yourself, Simon," she said, obviously unimpressed. "I'm home because I choose to be home. If I wanted to be out, I'd be out."

"I didn't say you didn't want to be out. I just figured you'd like to be out with the right kind of man and as far as I'm concerned, that's gotta be me."

"Don't flatter yourself, Simon," she told me. "I don't imagine that the right man would call me asking me about my dilly."

"I wasn't asking you about your dilly," I answered.

"Well, whose dilly were you asking about?"

Silence.

She knew she had me. What the heck was I going to say? If I was asking about her dilly, I wouldn't even have known. Why did I bother with the dilly approach anyway? What the heck *was* the dilly approach? It didn't matter. I was had and she was the only one who could save me.

"Are you still there?" she asked.

I didn't even get to answer.

"Hold on a second," she said. "I have another call."

Whew, I thought, collecting myself. *That was too close.*

Usually a guy hates when a woman has to take that dreaded "other call." The other call could be anything. Maybe she left her purse at work and she'd ask you to take her to the office because she didn't want to risk driving without her license. Maybe she hit the lottery and she needed a ride to cash in her ticket so she could take you on a vacation to some island with nude beaches and super-models who needed help with their tanning lotion.

Or maybe it was the guy she had plans with on the same Thursday night you just happened to call.

That's how it always worked. The last time I was on an island with a woman and some sunscreen was with Amber. And she was at least two hundred pounds from being a su-permodel.

"Simon," she said, coming back to the line. "Maybe a date wouldn't be so bad."

"Great," I answered, surprised. "I can pick you up in an hour."

"Why don't we meet somewhere?" she asked.

"I don't mind picking you up."

"I'm about to run out, so I'll meet you," she told me. "We can meet at the BET Jazz restaurant."

"Okay," I said, turning off the tube. "See you at about nine."

I hurried to my bedroom to dress. Eve wasn't the type you went casual with. She dressed. And unlike Stuart, my wardrobe had considerable limits. Searching the racks was pretty useless, especially since my racks were highlighted by only five hangers. Two of the hangers featured four pairs of jeans on one and five pairs of slacks on the other—two light, two dark and a neutral pair. My favorite hanger held two oversized football jerseys. And the one to right end held three oxford shirts, all of them white with button-down collars. A hanger to the far left of the closet held my black funeral suit. Though the funeral suit fit well and made the most of my abundant proportions, it was a little too formal for a quickie date with Eve. I decided on the neutral slacks with a white shirt and blazed to the restaurant.

Eve was a numbers lady. Which meant, among other things, that she watched the clock as much as she watched her wallet. She was going to be on time and I was determined to beat her there. When a guy could hit a date spot first and scope the place out, he had a major upper hand. A quick stroll to the bathroom would tell the full story. If you were with a woman you'd prefer not to be seen with, you could bail out before you ever got seated. And if you wanted to be seen, an early arrival could ensure that you were there before she was seated. That way, you could be led to a spot with her on your arm.

Unfortunately, she was seated by the time I hit the door. The hostess, who should have been making a living off of her beautiful looks, led me to the table and offered me a menu. Eve was stunning. She sat there in a hot little black dress and it was as if a beam of light shone down upon her. I felt like a guest at an E! Television fashion shoot.

She looked at her watch.

"Good timing, Simon. One hour on the nose."

"I aim to please," I replied, sitting across from her. "How's the menu?"

"I'm not really all that hungry," she casually stated. "Why don't we grab a burger and hit a club or something?"

"I was actually hoping we could talk a little," I said,

searching the menu. "This is a nice spot. And the food was pretty good last time I was here."

"They don't have burgers and you can't dance here."

"Noted," I said, standing and reaching for her hand. "Let's roll out."

With the restaurant in my rearview mirror, we hung a right on Tenth Street and headed across town toward Southwest D.C. She wanted to go to a club called Nation's, which was a little out of my league. From what I'd been told, Nation's was a players club. It was a spot where street-level drug dealers *played* with their colleagues, their women and their clientele in an environment that was all party. Guns and attitudes were left at home. Casual-cool was the dress of the day, which suited me fine. No tailored suits or freshly polished shoes. The club was a jeans and Timberland boots type of spot. The music was loud. A mix of hip-hop and D.C.'s home-grown, polyrhythmic go-go. By all accounts the women were wild, willing and full of life. That alone made it a hit with many older guys who wanted to pick up younger ladies looking for a good time.

D.C.'s night life was highlighted by clubs where style took precedent over substance. A decent guy could go to a club and count on being turned down at least six times by women who refused to dance because they "didn't like that record." That wasn't always bad. But it made no sense that many of the same women who literally hated a record just moments earlier, or were too tired to move, could be found enthusiastically shaking their groove things to the same record with some other guy who had a better suit, sharper shoes or a snappier ride in the parking lot than me. Who knows why they lied about hating a record or being too tired to dance? Hadn't these women learned anything from Nancy Reagan? What ever happened to "Just Say No"?

I was about to find out.

As we walked toward the club, a frail guy with flaming red hair, a huge black hat and an equally black outfit approached us. Knowing that I was about to hear about his rotten day, I reached in my pocket hoping to find a quarter. I didn't usually deal with panhandlers, because so many of them took your hard earned cash just to enliven their drinking, drug and smoking habits. But I'd be the first to admit there were times when dropping a quarter in a cup beat listening to a lie about much-needed bus fare or a meal that would never be purchased. I quickly realized a nice lie sometimes had its advantages.

Especially when a gun was being poked in your side.

When it hit me that we were being robbed, my first reaction was to hit the ground for cover. I'd never been held up before and wasn't exactly sure how the whole thing worked. On TV, some crazed lunatic always told you to put your hands in the air or to count to a hundred. The creative guys ordered you to count backward from a hundred while insisting that you not look at them. And the really creative guys jumped in your car while you were at a drive-through, forced you to order their lunch and then took your money and your car after dropping you off at your front door. My robber fell somewhere between creative and creatively absurd.

To my surprise, he said nothing and handed me a note.

I didn't know what to do, but the gun in my side reminded me to keep my wits about me. In the midst of the most frightening moment of my life, when a nice loud scream would have been a preference, I was about to read. I was scared beyond belief, but there was no way I could show it. Especially in front of Eve, who was now standing behind me with her arms locked around me.

"What does it say?" she said, trembling.

"It says he has a gup and that he's not afraid to use it," I whispered, nervously.

"A gup? What's a gup?" she asked, digging her nails into my arm.

"I don't know," I answered, turning toward him. "What's a gup?" I asked him.

He just grimaced and poked the gun in my side more forcefully.

"O-o-h," I said, my head slowly nodding. "It means he has a gun."

"Are you saying the guy who's robbing us can't spell?" she asked, clamping my arm like a vise. Then, suddenly, she let go, snatched the note from me and started to yell at him.

"You want to take my money and you can't even spell?! Do you know how hard I work?! You need to carry yourself somewhere and learn how to spell before you walk up here and try to rob somebody!"

"Ch-ch-chill out, Eve," I said, starting to sweat. "The man's got a gup."

"I don't care what he has!" she yelled. "He's not getting a dime of my money!"

Then she hit him with it. The patented, soul-sister

purse swing. After the bottom of her tiny purse hit the left side of his face, I felt the weapon jerk away from my side. And when her purse fell flush with his other cheek, he ran off as fast as I wanted to. It's moments like these that define a man and his legacy. And because I didn't want my legacy to be solely defined by my knees, which were *still* shaking, I had to make a move.

But I needed him to get far away enough first.

"Hey!" I yelled, gathering myself and starting to give chase. "Come back here!"

My only hope was that he hadn't heard me and that his fear of Eve would keep him running. I didn't want him to come back. Didn't want to catch him. And didn't want Eve to know or even sense that all I wanted was to get somewhere and down a strong, stiff drink.

"Simon!" she yelled, as I slowly jogged. "Come back. It's not worth it."

"Are you sure?" I asked, turning around.

"Of course," she said, grabbing my arm. "You're such a man."

"I am?" I asked, surprised.

"Did you ever see *Take The Money and Run?*" she asked.

"The Woody Allen movie," I replied, still catching my breath.

"Yes," she said, reaching inside her purse. "Woody used a holdup note just like the guy who tried to rob us," she remarked, pulling out a tiny napkin. "And he misspelled gun too," she added.

"That's right," I recalled.

"But you really handled it," she said, dabbing the sweat

from my brow. "It just made me feel so safe," she said, placing her hand in mine. "A woman likes feeling safe when she's out with a man."

I knew just what she meant. I'd never felt safer in my life. Eve not only managed to scare off a robber, but she also allowed me to save face with a sense of style and dignity that only a classy, tough lady could muster. As we strolled toward the club, my heart slowed and my head cleared. It happened so fast that it almost seemed like it hadn't happened at all. We'd almost been robbed! But Eve saved the day *and* preserved my legacy. The robber was just lucky that she'd beaten me to the punch. I might not have been carrying a weapon like Eve's purse, but I would have worn him out.

Even if he did have a "gup."

When we hit the door of Nation's, we weren't even frisked by the burly bouncers. As soon as they saw Eve, we were waved in and greeted with smiles and offered drinks. We both opted for cranberry juice with a twist and made our way to a tiny table at the rear of the club. I was still a little on the shaky side. *What if he had pulled the trigger when Eve went off on him?* I wondered. She didn't seem fazed. It was as if she'd been through this a dozen times. How were we supposed to party after we'd almost been killed? And what if she knew I'd been more frightened than she was? I sized up every guy wearing black who passed like he was a suspect. I actually considered calling "America's Most Wanted" when I left the club. But Eve wasn't having it. She was ready for action. I just hoped we were ready for the same type of action.

"So tell me what happened with you and football," she requested. "Did you ever get that tryout with the Redskins?"

"They called, but I wasn't ready," I admitted.

"What do you mean you weren't ready?" she asked, surprised. "That's all you used to talk about," she recalled. "All I need is a shot and I'm in the N-F-ing-L," she said, impersonating me.

"That was my line," I acknowledged, nodding my head. "But I don't even think about it anymore," I said. "You know how much I loved football, but I had a choice to make," I confessed. "You remember how much I wanted to go to a Super Bowl and just sit in the stadium?"

"That was your dream."

"You're right," I told her. "That *was* my dream," I added. "But I gave it up. I had to deal with a broken heart."

"*You* had a broken heart?" she said, sipping on her drink. "I'm so sorry," she added. "But you're over her now, aren't you?"

"Does anyone ever get over a broken heart?" I asked, looking her in the eye.

"Of course they do," she replied, smiling. "But just in case you didn't, if you tell me who she is, I'll take care of her for you," she joked.

"You don't know her," I lied. "And that's history," I said, wanting to keep the mood light. "How about a toast," I suggested, raising my glass. "To better endings."

"To better endings," she repeated. "Have you been here before?" she asked, half-swooning to the bass-heavy rap tune playing in the background.

"Hardly," I answered, watching two barely dressed beauties pass our table.

"Go ahead," she told me.

"Go ahead and what?" I asked, concerned.

"Go ahead and ask them to dance."

"I wasn't looking at them," I said, turning toward her.

"I didn't say you were looking at them," she went on. "Your eyes said it."

"You know, Eve, I never took you for the jealous type."

"And I never took you for the disrespectful type, Simon. But you are a man, so I can't say that I'm surprised."

She *couldn't* have been surprised. Unlike Stuart, I'd given up on the club scene years ago. Back then, women were out to dance. But now, the game was completely different. I couldn't believe what I was seeing. It was as if every woman in the place was trying to out-dress and out-attract every other woman. The guys just sat back in their chairs like they were modern-day kings holding court. The smoky haze that drifted about the room gave this big-city club a down-home, cozy feel. If a guy wanted to meet a woman, I could see Nation's was the spot.

Thankfully, it was also a spot where I could feel Eve out about our little brush with the wrong side of the law. I slowly raised a drink to my lips and took a quick sip. I'd read that a quick sip followed by a strong sniff exuded confidence. A trait that was a surefire turn-on for almost any woman.

She looked at me like I was crazy after the sniff, so I knew I had to say something.

"So, Eve," I started, worried. "That little incident didn't scare you too much, did it?"

"Maybe I was afraid for a teeny-weeny second, Simon, but you handled your business."

"I did?" I asked, surprised. "I mean, of course I did," I said, taking another quick sip, followed by another ridiculous sniff.

"Do you have a cold?" she asked, handing me a napkin.

"Nah," I told her. "I'm cool. I just wanted you to know that I had the situation under control. How about you and I dance?" I asked, trying to ease the mood.

"That's funny," she said, standing. "I've known you for years and I've never seen you dance."

"What's funnier is that I've known you for years and I've never seen you dance with your clothes on," I commented, harking back to her stripper days.

"Touché, Simon," she said, smiling. "Let's see what you've got."

That was a mistake. Seeing what I had on the dance floor was as painful as seeing a train after a late-night, snow-riddled derailment. It was a disaster. Eve still moved like Kit the stripper. And my moves (or lack thereof) more closely resembled those of an aging widow at a rundown retirement home. She twirled around like some kind of electric baton and I moved with the ferocity of an overused kitchen mop. The DJ saved me by throwing on some hip-hop mix of Chubby Checker's "The Twist." I could twist with the best of them, but it ultimately made little difference. The crowd broke out on some hybrid form of the Twist and the Jerk. I even saw one couple doing the Camel Walk, accented by something that vaguely resembled an opening number from Riverdance.

Eve, who was keen for this bass beat–driven travesty, somehow managed to incorporate the Twist, Jerk, Camel

Walk and Irish High-Step into one amazing series of dance moves. She was Debbie Allen, Rosie Perez and Paula Abdul all wrapped up in one.

When the song ended, my first reaction was to applaud. She must have sensed that I was about to make a complete fool of myself. "Okay," she said, grabbing my hand and leading me back to the table. "I see why you never let me see you dance."

"Yeah," I said, reaching for a chair. "Since I've put on this weight, I'm not what you'd call light on my feet," I admitted. "But it's okay, because I have bigger fish to fry."

"So you're a cook, are you?"

"You should know that," I reminded her. "We used to be quite a dish."

"That we were," she acknowledged.

"Speaking of cooking," I started. "What are you and your family planning for Thanksgiving?"

"We're at a club," she answered. "Who wants to talk about family?"

Then she reached over and laid a kiss on my lips that raced down my body and landed right in my lap. At least I thought it landed in my lap. When I looked down and noticed her hand exactly where I wanted it to be, I knew what was next.

"Why did you really call me?" she asked, rubbing gently.

"Well," I sighed. "I wanted to see you. I actually wanted to see you since the day you rode on my vehicle."

"If you play your cards right I'll ride your vehicle tonight," she whispered seductively.

"Strip poker sounds good to me," I said, remembering our old days.

"How about 'go fish,' " she said coldly.

"What's up?" I asked, noticing her hands folded on the table.

"I can't believe you think I would just sleep with you because you took me to Nation's," she whipped out. "I know why you called me and I'd respect you more if you said you were horny and you thought I was a good lay."

"I am horny and I *know* you're a great lay," I confessed.

She shot me a look that was more menacing than a Mike Tyson pre-fight stare down.

"But that's not why I called. Look, Eve," I started. "I've always liked you for who you were and not what you did," I said. "You're a beautiful woman and to tell the truth, I'm honored that you're even out with me," I added. "If we can at least try to get to know each other, you'll see I'm for real," I told her. "Just give me a shot and you'll see what's happening."

"And you think it's that easy?" she asked.

"I never said it was easy, but it'll only be as hard as you make it," I answered.

"Now I remember what I liked about you, Simon. You have this quiet confidence."

"It's not so quiet," I replied, smiling. "But I have to admit, you always brought out the best in me and I'd like to see you and have some real dates that don't end up in the bedroom."

"So you're saying if I offered you up right now you'd turn me down?" she asked.

"Are you calling me crazy?"

We laughed, and she reached for my hand.

"If you want to hang out, we can hang out," she said,

walking toward the door. "But I can't promise you I won't jump your bones from time to time."

"That'll work," I said as we reached the sidewalk. "You can jump my bones tonight if you really have to."

"I was going to until you said you didn't want to end up in the bedroom," she said, waving down a taxi. "You're still a sweetheart, Simon," she whispered, climbing in. "Call me tomorrow."

I didn't know what was crazier. The fact that I was so mesmerized that I let her jump in a taxi without offering her a ride home, or the fact that I put my foot so squarely in my mouth that I needed industrial-strength floss to scrape the leather out. I had to call it a tie. Especially when it hit me that my only response to, "Call me tomorrow," had been a supercorny "Count on it."

It didn't matter. Going home horny and knowing I had a shot with Eve was better than just going home horny and getting frustrated with the Spice Channel because they showed even less than I was getting.

And I wasn't getting anything.

At least not tonight.

chapter 5

Stuart, Lynn, Two Guys from New York and Barbra Streisand

Eight Minutes Later

Stuart

N

othing smacks harder than reality. Lynn was the perfect candidate for the trip. She wouldn't insist that we have a relationship and she wouldn't fall in love because of a free, exotic island trip. But what if she had a man? It was Thursday night, I'd called her two hours ago, and she still hadn't called me back. And I knew she wasn't home, because I'd called three more times. If a woman was running the streets on a Thursday night, you could bet she was running with some guy. I knew this to be true, because I was usually that guy. In D.C., weekends started on Thursday. And if you had even half a life, you'd been invited to or knew of some activity that could throw you in the mix with members of the opposite sex.

But me, I was the ultimate party man and I was stuck at home, watching the phone and wondering why it hadn't rung. None of my regular dates had called. The woman I'd met last week, who caught me with another woman the night before, *wouldn't* call. And I'd even called Simon and *he* was out. Which meant he probably had the upper hand on the date-for-Cancun sweepstakes. Maybe he was telling the truth about his girl Eve. They were probably waltzing around some swanky Georgetown boutique. She was modeling bikinis. He was smiling like Bill Clinton when Hillary's out of town. And they were finalizing plans for the big trip.

And, if the phone hadn't rung at that very moment, I'd have paged him and let him gloat. But maybe this call would put me right beside him.

"What up?" I answered, hoping it would be a woman who wasn't trying to sell something.

"What up?" a sultry voice replied. "What is it with men?" she asked. "You left two messages, Stuart. What's up with you?"

"Lynn," I said, trying to sound relaxed. "You just caught me. I was about to step out."

"Well don't let me hold you," she said casually. "I was merely returning your calls."

Damn. Why did she give up so easily? I wasn't going anywhere. At least not in my silk pajamas. It was almost midnight and I'd listened to Jill Scott's new album for three straight hours. Jill's music was deep and passionate, and it was exciting. She'd brought the house down at Chris Rock's season debut a few weeks ago, and now she was taking the country by storm, just like I was ready to take Lynn—by storm. Who cared if I had major work waiting for me tomorrow? She could have at least pretended to be interested in where I was going. But why would she? And why was she calling me at midnight, anyway?

"Lynn," I said, wanting to gain the upper hand. "It's late and you're obviously up. Why don't we go grab some coffee?"

"Coffee at midnight?" she asked. "I'll be up all night."

"That's what I was hoping," I remarked, grinning.

"I guess we could do some decaf," she answered. "Why don't we meet at Starbucks in Georgetown?"

"Why don't I pick you up and we'll ride together?" I asked.

"I'm in a cab, Stuart. Just meet me there in twenty minutes."

Great!

Twenty minutes was more than I needed. I zipped to my closet, which closely resembled a high-tech, motorized dry-cleaning retrieval line. My grandmother taught me all I needed to know about style and fashion. She had no use for walk-in closets and once told me, "You're a Worthington and we don't walk into closets. The closet comes to us."

"Casual," I stated into the tiny wall-mounted speaker.

A moment later, several racks of casual clothing arrived. Though they were decent enough, they were a little too sporty for what I had in mind.

"Late-evening casual."

Just seconds later, my collection of late-night casual slacks and sweaters was staring me straight in the face. I reached for a pair of pleated sandalwood-colored slacks and a matching cashmere V-neck sweater. Zelda, my wardrobe consultant, maintained my closet. She had a sizeable credit line to keep me ahead of the fashion curve and had full access to my closet on a twenty-four-hour, as-needed basis. She understood that clothes were my passion and never hesitated to remind me that anyone who worked as hard as I did deserved one vice. Over the years, my "vice" served me well, but tonight I was looking for immediate dividends.

I had to book Lynn for the Cancun trip.

By the time I made it to Starbucks, Lynn was in place. She sat at a booth reading a copy of D.C.'s weekly tell-all tabloid, the *Washington City Paper*. I approached her and before I even sat down she said, "Very good, Stuart. Twenty minutes on the dot."

"What makes you think it's me?" I asked, noticing that she hadn't even looked up from the paper.

"Boucheron," she said, moving the paper away from her face, "It's the only thing you wear during the fall."

"You remember that?" I asked, impressed.

"Cigar in spring. DKNY during summer. Boucheron in the fall. And we didn't last until winter, so I don't know what you wear then."

"We can do something about that," I said, reaching to kiss her hand.

"That depends on what you have in mind," she said, smiling. "By the way, you look nice."

"Thanks," I answered, reaching for a menu. "I hate to ask, but I have to. What are you doing out so late?"

"Are you suggesting that I have a curfew?"

"Not in those words. But, you're a *VP* and I'd imagine you're expected at the office pretty early."

"Aren't you?" she retorted.

"I set my own schedule," I bragged. "But I do have an early meeting tomorrow."

"So what are *you* doing out so late?" she asked.

"I couldn't catch you at home and I figured if you can't beat 'em, join 'em, so I'm here."

"Well, join me and don't worry about why I'm out so late," she said, winking. "Late can be good, you know."

"My thoughts exactly. What are you having?"

"A grande latte, with two shots."

"Good choice," I agreed. "In fact, I'm having that myself. I'll go pick it up."

"I already ordered," she told me.

"What made you think I wanted the same thing you wanted?"

"Maybe I wanted the same thing *you* wanted," she answered.

"What makes you think you knew what I wanted?" I asked, starting to stand.

"The same thing that made me know you'd meet me for coffee at midnight," she said, slyly.

That was too strong. Which is what I liked about Lynn. She affected me like no woman ever had and she played more head games than Tony's shrink on "The Sopranos." And within a matter of minutes, she had my mind racing: *I was the one who left her two messages and then asked her out, but she's saying she knew I would join her for coffee...*

Maybe she's saying that she was going to ask me out, but I beat her to the punch... Which couldn't be the case because when I told her I was on my way out, she was cool with it... That's what she said. Isn't it?

"Sir?"

"Yeah," I answered, still in a fog.

"I believe these are for you," the server said, reaching across the counter. "I don't mean to rush you, but there's a line."

I turned around and headed back toward our booth. I couldn't help but notice that the shop was quite full. After a night of heavy drinking, heavy dancing and for those who got lucky, heavy petting, a good cup of coffee can work wonders.

"Two grande lattes, with four shots," I said, sitting down.

"So let's get down to brass tacks," she said, taking a sip. "Why did you ask me out for coffee at midnight?"

I just looked at her and wondered how she knew. How could she have known? While I was standing in line, that's all I thought of. When I walked back to the table it was on my mind. And even as I took my first sip, I wondered, *Why did you ask her out at midnight?* And more important, *Why did she accept?*

"I already told you," I replied, gathering myself. "You were out, I was going out, and I figured it'd be nice to see you."

"So you see me," she said, again sipping. "Does that mean we're done?"

"We're done if you want to be done. But if you wanted to be done, you wouldn't be here," I answered, before winking at her.

"Well, aren't we presumptuous," she commented.

"No. W-e-e just had something to run across you," I said, thinking about the trip.

"And it couldn't wait. You just had to tell me tonight."

"Tonight's as good a time as any."

"This better be good, Stuart," she casually remarked. "Go ahead."

"Well, me and a group of friends—"

"Excuse me," interrupted a well-coifed guy, leaning in.

"But table space is kind of limited," said a blond-haired guy standing beside him.

"So if you don't mind," the first one added, stroking his gel-laced black locks.

"We'd like to join you," the other chimed in.

"Actually, we were in the middle of a conversation," I said, staring them down.

"Great," the first one said.

"So were we," the blond added.

"So it really shouldn't be a problem," they said together. "Would you mind scooting over?"

I minded, but it didn't matter. Lynn was at ease and actually seemed to welcome the company.

"We'll just be a second," the black-haired one said, sitting down. "I'm Craig and this is my partner, Josh," he went on, referring to the blond. "This is such nice weather. Can you believe Thanksgiving is just a week away?" he asked. "I bet you two have really big plans. And might I say, that is just fab," he said of Lynn's dress.

"I'm glad someone noticed," she replied, seeming to take a stab at me.

"Oh, he noticed," Josh told her. "But he looks pretty good himself," he said, winking at me.

"Josh!" his black-haired partner scoffed.

"Relax, sweetheart," he casually replied. "He's spoken for."

"No, he's not," Lynn said, smiling.

Josh then winked at me again, which caused Craig to kick him.

"Okay, Craig," he said, staring at him. "I'm just kidding."

"So what brings you two out tonight?" Craig asked, sipping his coffee.

"A little dance or a little romance?" Josh asked, edging closer toward me.

"If you guys hurry up with your coffee, maybe we can get to both," I said tersely.

"We were actually thinking about a little Celebrity," Craig remarked, sipping his coffee.

"Hold up," I started. "I know you guys didn't interrupt us to talk about Mini-Me."

"He didn't mean a 'little' celebrity," Josh giggled.

"I think he meant the game Celebrity," Lynn told me.

"That's even worse," I shot back. "Do you think I met you here to play games?"

"You're a *man*, honey," Josh gushed. "That means you're an expert at playing games."

Knowing he was a man, I couldn't help but give him a cold, hard stare. But when he again winked at me and then blew me a kiss, I considered that talking about Mini-Me or even playing a game about him wouldn't be a bad idea.

"I love Celebrity," Lynn said, easing the suddenly tense mood. "Why don't we play?"

"Look, fellas," I interrupted. "This has been great, but

we have a few things to discuss here, so if you don't mind—"

"Of course we don't mind," Josh said, smiling. "Let's play."

"Boys against girls?" Craig asked, reaching for Josh's hand.

I looked around the table. Boys versus girls? There were three guys and one very beautiful woman. When I saw their hands locked together and their eyes melting like two chocolate-lovers trapped in a Godiva store, I got the picture. I just wondered how they figured out who the girl was.

"Okay, Craig," Lynn said, reaching for a napkin. "You and I will play against Stuart and Josh."

"But I thought we were playing boys against girls," Josh whined.

"Oh, Josh," Craig snapped.

"This is how you play, Stuart," Lynn started. "Write down ten names on a piece of paper, fold them up and put them in this bowl."

"Then you pick one out and give your teammate a clue about the name," Craig told me.

"Only you can't say any part of the person's name," said Josh, scribbling on a napkin. "By the way," he whispered. "Has anyone ever told you that you bear an amazing resemblance to Denzel. When he was much younger, of course."

My grandmother once told me that, but I never bought it. And hearing it from Josh all but confirmed it. With his badly bleached hair and his dollar-store plastic coat, he wouldn't have known Denzel if he'd walked in and ordered a round of lattes for the house.

"So if you said, 'J.J.'s mother, Florida—' " Lynn added, writing on her paper.

"The answer would be Esther Rolle," Craig went on. "And if you said, 'Dynomite!' "

"The answer would be Jimmie Walker and not J.J. because J.J. wasn't a celebrity, he was a character," Josh chimed in, still writing.

"I get it," I said, pulling out my Mont Blanc rollerball. "I write down some celebrity's name, we give each other hints and we have to guess who it is."

"Right," Lynn answered. "Each round lasts a minute and your score is based on how many you guess correctly."

"Everybody ready?" Craig said, excited.

"This is so much fun," Josh remarked. "You guys can go first."

Craig gave the hints while Lynn answered. I truly didn't want to play a parlor game with a real, live version of the cackling cartoon mynah birds, Heckle and Jeckle.

"Thriller," Craig stated.

"Michael Jackson," she answered.

"Mookie," he said.

"Mookie Wilson, the baseball player," she guessed.

"Remember," he reminded her. "I can't use the name. Okay. Try this. *Do the Right Thing.*"

"Spike Lee?" she asked.

"Yes!"

"Why didn't you say *Malcolm X*?" she asked, concerned. "That was a much better film than *Do the Right Thing.*"

"You're wasting our time, sweetheart," he said, drawing another sheet. " 'Material Girl,' " he added.

"Madonna!" she replied.

"Time!" Josh piped up. "They only got three. They don't stand a chance do they, honey?" he asked, looking toward me.

"Who the hell you calling 'honey'?" I fired back.

"Yes! I love to see a man with spunk," Josh told me. "Let's get it on, honey," he said, blowing me a kiss.

"Star Wars," I said, giving him a hint.

"R2-D2?" he guessed.

"The director," I added.

"George Lucas!" he answered proudly.

"Latina singer," I said.

"Selena," Josh answered.

"I didn't say dead Latina singer," I remarked. "Latina singer with a nice ass."

"Ricky Martin!" he and Craig exclaimed, slapping each other high five.

"Guys don't have nice asses," I said, frustrated. "Latin-*a*. She played Selena in the movie."

"Excuse me, mister," Craig said, pointing at me.

"But men absolutely have nice asses," Josh confessed. "In fact, yours is kind of cute, isn't it, hon?" he asked Lynn.

"We noticed while you were in line," Craig said, smiling. "I hope you don't mind," he said, turning to Lynn.

As with Josh's question, she said nothing and just winked at me. I didn't know if that meant I had a nice ass, or if she didn't mind if they had checked out my so-called nice ass. And what if she thought their asses were nicer than mine? Is that something a guy should feel threatened by?

"By the way, I believe the Latina singer would be Jennifer Lopez," Josh finally answered.

"Good," I stated, reaching for another paper. "She wore ruby-red slippers in *The Wizard of Oz.*"

"Oh my God, oh my God, oh my God," he started. "Miss Judy Garland. The queen of cinema. The greatest singer ever."

"Excuse me, sir," Craig said, interrupting our turn. "But she's no Diana Ross."

"Diana Ross," Lynn said, truly ignoring any rules of good gamesmanship. "What about Aretha Franklin?"

"As long as we're talking singers, I'd like to put my vote in for Barbra Streisand," I interrupted.

Josh and Craig then looked at me and, without saying a word, stood up.

"We really don't appreciate the stereotype," Craig said, wrapping his neck with a scarf.

"That's like saying that you people like James Brown," Josh told us.

"We people do like James Brown," Lynn and I answered together.

"Fine," Craig said, walking away.

"You can like him without us," Josh added.

And then they left. It was as sudden as it was surprising. I initially wasn't interested in the stupid game, but it had turned out okay. I looked at the paper on the table and tried to make some sense of it. I really did like Barbra Streisand. I'd heard that gay guys had a thing for her, but I never knew it was a stereotype. And though it was clear that Josh was hitting on me, I didn't see them as gay guys. I just saw them as guys. What bothered me most was not their leaving because of a misunderstanding, but their leaving with the game all tied up. Even though Josh screwed the whole thing up by proclaiming Judy Garland as the ultimate diva, I'm pretty sure we would have won.

"Well," Lynn said, starting to stand. "This has been one of the more interesting evenings I've ever had."

"Yeah," I said, helping her with her jacket. "Josh was trying to pick me up and you and Craig almost beat us in Celebrity."

"We would have killed you guys," she replied, walking toward the door.

"Maybe," I answered, opening the door. "Especially since you were basking in your fifteen minutes of fame."

"What are you talking about?" she asked, walking toward a waiting cab.

"You were out with me," I reminded her. "That qualifies you for celebrity status on some level."

"Cute, Stuart," she said, sliding in and lowering the window. "Speaking of celebrities," she whispered. "Has anyone ever told you that you look like a young Denzel?"

She then winked, blew me a kiss and pulled off into the night. I didn't get to sell her on the trip, but the evening clearly wasn't a total loss. In fact, Lynn made the whole thing right inside of five seconds. Sometimes the best-laid plans fall flat in your face.

And other times it doesn't matter one bit.

Denzel, I thought proudly, strutting toward my car. *My grandmother must have been right.*

Simon, Stuart and the Kids

Friday—The Next Afternoon

Simon

'd spent the night wondering about Eve. Where she was. What she was doing. And who she was doing it with. Did she have to rescue another date from a robber gone mad, like she'd done with me? It didn't much matter. Our time alone, albeit brief, had helped me to realize how much I missed having a woman in my life. With her good sense of humor, sense of independence and resolve, and a body that could give a *Sports Illustrated* swimsuit photographer a chubby, she could definitely fill that void. And Eve and I would probably be making plans right now if Stuart and I hadn't committed to our latest task. As we sat in an amazingly cramped office, I considered our venture: we'd driven deep into the toughest ward of the nation's capital, Southeast, to mentor two inner-city teenaged boys.

Did you get my message last night?" Stuart asked, glancing at his watch.

"Yeah," I answered, thumbing through a magazine. "But I was caught up, if you know what I mean."

"Caught up with what?"

"Me, Eve and a little spot known as Nation's."

"*You* went to Nation's?" he asked, surprised.

"I just said I went to Nation's, didn't I?" I replied, casually turning a page.

"What the hell did you do at Nation's?"

"I danced my fat ass off," I said, laughing.

"I can't believe it," he told me. "You're swinging at the Nexus Gold Room and I was stuck at a coffee house with Lynn and two nuts from N.Y.C."

"Two nuts from New York would have been better than what I had to deal with," I confessed.

"If you were hanging with a honey who dragged you to Nation's, the only thing you had to put up with was her wanting to be on top when she dragged you home," he laughed.

"It didn't get to that," I said, high-fiving him. "But it could have."

"Well, did it get to booking her for the trip?" he asked.

"It's not even about the trip," I answered. "I'm feeling her and I want to make something happen."

"You can make something happen," he scoffed. "But while you're trying to play Romeo, I'm booking Lynn for the trip," he added. "You don't want a wife. All you need is a warm body to stretch out with in Cancun."

"Last time I checked, Amber and Sonya from last year were *two and a half* warm bodies," I reminded him. "And you remember where that got us."

"Where exactly *did* that get you?" a stern, husky voice asked.

"Oh," I said, sitting up. "Mrs. Platz. He was just asking me for directions, since I'm a vehicle operator and all."

"You're a bus driver, Washington," she commented, looking through a folder.

"I've been trying to tell him that," Stuart chimed in.

"Gentlemen, why are you wasting my time today?" she asked, staring us down like a police interrogator.

"We're not exactly wasting your time," I answered.

"Of course we're not," Stuart said, smiling. "We just thought it was time that we pitched in."

"Yeah," I told her. "We're trying to keep it real."

"Up in the field," Stuart quickly added, raising a true soul-brother fist.

"I don't care what kind of field you're trying keep it real in," Mrs. Platz told us. "You bobos wouldn't know what to do if one of these at-risk be-boppers snatched your wallet."

"I'd whip his little ass," Stuart said convincingly.

"I don't think he meant it quite like that," I interrupted, poking Stuart in the side.

"Of course I didn't," he said, turning on the charm. "I'd just grab him and shake him real good."

"And you think that's better?" she asked, unimpressed.

"Better than whipping his ass?" I asked, concerned.

"I'd whip that ass too," she said, now smiling.

I didn't want to whip anybody's ass. Even when that non-spelling robber hit me and Eve up the night before, I didn't want to whip his ass. I just wanted his ass to run faster than mine. But what if Stuart and Mrs. Platz were right? At-risk kids could be a challenge. And why we opted for this challenge escaped me. If memory served me correctly, it started with Stuart's near-insane theory that women were attracted to guys who tutored children. It then moved to women liking guys who mentored kids. And the final incarnation was Stuart's claim that, "Chicks want men who can handle screwed-up kids like theirs." I'd always thought a noble reason like halfway wanting to make a positive impact on someone else's life was the ticket.

Apparently, I was wrong.

"Mr. Worthington," Mrs. Platz started. "You have a grip on the situation."

Stuart just smiled and nodded.

"But you, Washington," she said, turning toward me. "You're probably one of those cuckoo liberals who believes that these little knuckleheads need counseling and coddling instead of a good, swift kick in the pants."

"I'm not kicking anybody in the pants," I told her.

"You're in over your head here, Washington, and that's your problem," she told me. "And that's the problem with these kids. They need a kick in the pants," she said, reaching in her desk and retrieving a glass. "They *want* to be kicked in the pants," she added, pouring from a silver-plated flask. "It shows that you care. It's all they know."

"I don't think that's how we want to carry it," Stuart said, coming to his senses.

"We just want to help," I told her.

"Help schmelp," she said, guzzling her drink. "You want to help?" she asked. "I got two losers you can help. B.L. and Marc. Take your pick. It won't even take you ten minutes to want to kick both of them in the pants."

She then handed us two folders.

"B.L.'s the oldest one," she started. "He's a real piece of work."

"Good-looking kid," Stuart told her.

"They say that Attila the Hun wasn't hard on the eyes either," she said, sipping and smiling.

"Are they brothers?" I asked, noticing their resemblance.

"Calling them brothers would be a disservice to brothers everywhere," Platz added, still drinking. "They have the same momma, but who the hell knows who the daddy is."

"How old is Marc?" I asked, flipping through his folder.

"Old enough to figure out your ATM password and clean you out within an hour," she answered.

"And what about B.L.?" asked Stuart.

"He won't waste time with your password," she started. "He'll just rob you blind."

"Great," I said, looking toward Stuart.

"We'll take them," Stuart chimed in.

"This isn't a carryout. They have to like you first," she stated. "But my thinking is that they'll see you as an easy mark, so you shouldn't have any problem."

"They have to like *us*?" Stuart asked. "They need us. We're the ones who should get to decide on them."

"Like I said, Worthington. *You* get it," she agreed, starting to stand. "But some needle-nuts liberal passed a bill that says these little panty-wipes have to accept you as a mentor."

"So *we're* about to be inspected?" I asked, concerned.

"Don't sound so worried, Washington," she said, opening the door. "The little nudnicks are right down the hall. I'll snatch them up, and if you don't cut the mustard, my sister works over at animal control. Dogs don't have to like you."

"Hey, Simon," Stuart whispered, as her heavy footsteps plopped down the hall. "I hope they like us. I hate dogs."

The 60-Day Rule

Weeks 3-4

The Realm of Reality

We'd been dating about a month when I picked Leigh up for dessert one evening. When she answers the door, her face is plastered in a pasty green beauty masque. About twenty minutes later, she strolls in wearing a pair of floppy jeans and her hair is pulled back into a ponytail. Her nails are even shorter than mine. She's not wearing any make-up: no lipstick. No eye shadow or blush. She's totally minimalist. A look that every guy hates. Over ice cream, she said she actually *wanted* me to see her at her worst. And that's when it hit me. The first two weeks... they were all show. We'd lasted a month and the glam was gone. She was now a woman. A real woman—short nails, green beauty masque and all. Suffice it to say, we'd entered a point of no return—the Realm of Reality.

Trevor W. Livingston, M.D.
The Married Doctor

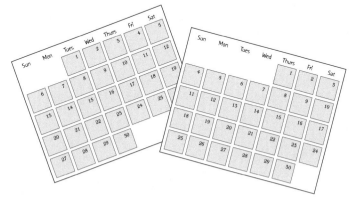

chapter 1

The Married Buddies, Trevor and Rod, Plot a Scheme

Fourteen Seconds Later

Simon

Trevor and Rod often hooked up at Butler's, D.C.'s top cigar bar, and talked about everything under the sun. Butler's was a unique combination of a classic, neo-conservative, political bully-pulpit and a New Age, new money, smoke-filled hideaway. Old-school political hacks and entrenched, seasoned lawmakers dominated the lounges and private humidors that made Butler's a favorite lunch and martini spot. Their subordinates, who seemed to have an eerie disdain for their bosses and the good ole boys network that kept them in power, made Butler's a hip nightspot. Ambitious young attorneys mingled with hotshot residents and MDs. Hip-hop business types exchanged business cards and CDs with the ample press corps that relaxed on the inviting red sofas. And horny, middle-aged men who broke bread with attractive, younger women sat mesmerized, hoping that their companion had a presidential intern's clue of how to really handle a Cuban Macanudo.

I learned of Rod and Trevor's meetings at Butler's because Rod one day rode my route and told me how truly neurotic Trevor really was. We spent an entire evening exchanging Trevor-and-Stuart stories. Because of our near-legendary single status, Stuart and I had evolved into best friends, while Trevor and Rod reached out to each other. It wasn't that either of us particularly cared for one over the other, in fact, it was quite the opposite. Coming up, Stuart and Trevor, who could now put the Hatfields and McCoys to shame, were the best of friends. And when Trevor left for college and returned from spring break with Leigh, Stuart was livid. Rod and I had become tight, but when Grace entered the picture, I was eventually phased out as his best friend. Interestingly, Trevor and Rod liked each other the least. But the moment they tied the knot, they somehow became fast friends and Stuart and I were forced into friendship.

What we hated was watching our buddies get clobbered by one of the oldest, cruelest and, quite frankly, most effective male rites of passage, the "rules of engagement."

Guys who were hooked up, shacking up or otherwise "engaged" in some level of cohabitation or key-sharing with a significant other, generally weren't allowed to fraternize with guys who didn't have a girlfriend, a wife, a fiancée or some other mate with a leash as long and formidable as theirs. If your buddy was dating a woman, you were allowed to be an unconditional best friend. But when the relationship progressed, and if you were still as hopelessly single as Stuart and me, the friendship quickly faded. And it was no mistake.

Wives didn't want you around their husbands, unless of course it was under their roof. They knew you were a decent guy and decent guys had a not-so-cute way of attracting decent women, who had decent girlfriends who wouldn't mind hanging out with your buddy even if he was married. So, your calls to your ex-best buddies went unreturned, because their new wives somehow always forgot to pass on the messages. And since guys hated it when a call went unreturned, they started to think that their best friend had gotten uppity and was so caught up in marital bliss that he'd cut off the partner who actually convinced him to get married when his feet had gotten so cold he couldn't even slip into his shoes.

Stuart went through it with Trevor. And I went through it with Rod. The rules of engagement hit hard. I missed the close friendship Rod and I once shared. But I doubted that Rod and Trevor shared the same warm and fuzzy feelings.

He's an idiot," Trevor said, lifting a Bud Light.

"Stuart's no more an idiot than Simon," Rod insisted. "They're just not focused when it comes to women."

"They're almost thirty and they have absolutely nothing going on," Trevor interrupted. "It's not as if they have some compelling outside interest that would keep them from finding Ms. Right."

"Their outside interest is getting laid," Rod told him.

"That's not the worst interest in the world," Trevor said. "But why can't they parlay that into something more substantial than a series of one-night stands that go nowhere?"

"What's the rush?" Rod asked.

"The rush is that Thanksgiving's a week away and the trip is a month after that," Trevor remarked.

"And?"

"And they don't have dates for either one, Rod," Trevor reminded him. "How long is this supposed to go on?" he asked. "Hey," he said, noticing Rod staring vacantly into the distance. "Are you here with me?"

"Yeah," he slowly answered. "Trevor," he started. "Have you ever thought what it would be like if you and Leigh weren't together?"

"I'd be fine," Trevor answered. "But it's not like I really want to think about it."

"What if she were without you. How do you think that would be?" Rod asked.

"She wouldn't last five minutes," he answered. "You know that's how things work. Women don't fare well without their men. So if you're thinking about leaving Grace and the girls you can just forget about it."

"Yeah," Rod said, shaking his head as if he were in doubt. "I guess I wouldn't want to leave them."

"I hope you're not letting Stuart and Simon rub off on you, my friend," Trevor told him. "You've got a great situation. Grace is a real keeper," he added. "Am I missing something here?" he asked, concerned. "If I didn't know better, I'd say something's eating at you."

"I was just thinking," Rod sighed. "Maybe they're not ready."

"Maybe we need to get them ready," Trevor told him.

"Not that again," Rod begged.

"Not what again?" Trevor started. "We have wives who know nice women," he said, taking a sip. "And Leigh thinks she's a matchmaker, so I say we do it."

"Do you remember Leigh's last shot at hooking them up?"

"How was she supposed to know?"

"How could she not have known?" Rod asked, clipping a cigar and handing it to Trevor. "They showed up to your dinner party with home detention bracelets."

"I thought they were just clunky ankle bracelets," Trevor said, lighting up. "And Leigh thought they were some sort of medical implements," he added.

"How does a doctor—and in Leigh's case I use the term loosely—anyway, how does she not know that they weren't medical things? Did she think they had twin freak ankle fractures or something?" Rod asked, reaching for Trevor's lighter.

"They weren't that bad," Trevor reminded him. "In fact, I found them quite attractive."

"Attractive?!" Rod exclaimed. "They were on parole, Trevor!"

"They were victims of America's twisted, liberal criminal justice system."

"When you've spent time in the hooch for embezzlement, they force you to surrender your victim status," Rod answered.

"Okay, point well taken," Trevor said, puffing on his stogie. "This time she'll get it right. We'll get a background check, credit check, the works," he continued. "We'll know every guy they've ever dated, slept with or even dreamed about, if that makes you happy."

"We don't need to do this, Trevor," Rod insisted. "They say they have a line on dates for the trip," he added. "So why don't we let them do their thing?"

"Because we let them do their thing last year and their *things* ate us out of house and home. And besides," he went on, "it could be said that they're our buddies and we'd be remiss in our responsibilities if we had a chance to help them and didn't."

"Maybe you're right," Rod considered. "And Leigh does know some fine women."

"Even if they are on parole," Trevor joked, tipping his drink.

"And that's something I don't get," Rod said, tapping out his ashes.

"What's that, Rod?"

"How does someone like Leigh meet two hotties like them?"

"They were in some encounter group together," Trevor answered. "You know Leigh, she meets someone who's into that New Age nonsense and they're instantly best friends."

"That's definitely Leigh," Rod said, smiling. "But what really spooks me is your being so casual about having those two crooks in your spot. When did Mister Conservative, 'God bless Rudy Giuliani,' get so soft on crime?"

"They were classic white collar criminals and I'm a Republican, Rod," Trevor started. "Think about it," he added, proudly raising his cigar. "We're practically family."

chapter 8

Meanwhile, Back with the Kids

Simon

S tuart," I whispered, as we heard footsteps approaching, "No more of that 'I'd whip his little ass' crap."

"Look, Simon," he answered, as we inspected a picture of superlawyer Johnnie Cochran speaking to a crowded audience. "It's not like I'm into kids anyway. But if doing this gives us an upper hand with the ladies, it's worth it," he told me. "And for the record, if they're big and they screw with my wallet I'll whip their *big* asses."

"So it's like that, huh, man?" a raspy voice asked. "You got a thing for asses."

"That's probably why he's hanging with the big fella," another voice quipped. "He's got a w-h-o-l-e lot of ass."

In less than a heartbeat we understood Mrs. Platz's claim. B.L. and Marc. Young, black, hard-core at-risk males. Two young brothers who were card-carrying members of a most dubious subgroup—America's *Least* Wanted.

"Enough with the ass jokes," Mrs. Platz said, arranging a set of chairs in a circle. "Shut up, sit down and let's get this catastrophe on the road," she added, pulling out a cigarette. "I'm headed down to Wayson's Corner to play bingo in an hour."

"I'm Simon," I said, reaching out to shake their hands.

"You're fat," the younger one answered, laughing.

"I'm gonna like this little guy," I said, trying to save face.

"The name is Worthington. Stuart Worthington," Stuart said, reaching for the older one's hand.

"Worthington?" he asked, sounding offended. "What the hell kind of name is Worthington?"

"It's the kind of name that says he had a daddy and that he knows where the hell his daddy is," Mrs. Platz interrupted. "But you wouldn't know anything about that, now would you?" she asked, blowing smoke about the room.

Her smoke was symbolic. We were in a haze. I couldn't believe she hit him with that. In a flash, I felt just like Stuart. But the only ass I wanted to whip was *hers*. Mrs. Platz was a case study of classic burnout. She hated us for even being there, which somehow forced her to do some work. And it was clear she had little, if any, feelings for the very people she was there to serve, B.L. and Marc. But Stuart was quick and probably just as mean-spirited. He was a comeback machine. And there was little doubt she was about to know it.

"Actually I don't know where my father is," he said, looking at B.L. "He left my mom when I was three. But I understand," he surmised. "Moms was pretty screwed up," he added, pointing toward Mrs. Platz. "Just like her."

Both Marc and B.L. wasted little time in laughing and then licking their tongues at Mrs. Platz, who, amazingly, seemed completely unfazed by Stuart's comments.

"Good for him," she shot back, referring to Stuart's dad. "He didn't have to deal with you or your screwed-up momma."

"Are you talking about his momma?" I asked, starting to stand.

"I'll talk about your momma too, if you don't sit your big ass down," she said, puffing on her cigarette.

"We don't have to deal with this," B.L. said, his voice strained.

"Yeah, just send us back to the receiving home," Marc begged.

"Yes you do have to deal with it," she reminded them. "You little punks will deal with whatever I dish out, when I dish it out, and how I dish it out and don't forget it."

"I think we get your point, Mrs. Platz," I remarked. "Why don't you give us a few minutes with the boys—"

"Who the hell you callin' 'boy,' fat boy?" Marc exclaimed, jumping up.

"Who the hell you callin' 'fat boy,' boy?" Stuart shot back, rising from his seat.

"Who you callin' 'boy,' *Worthington*?!" B.L. said, clenching his fist and standing toe to toe with Stuart. "Don't no-body talk to my baby brother like that."

"It's cool," I said, grabbing Stuart's arm. "I don't think anybody meant anything. I was just asking a question."

"And you got an answer," Mrs. Platz said, standing. "I'm not missing bingo for this," she went on, reaching for her purse. "Just drop them over at the receiving home when you're done with them," she added, throwing on her coat. "Call me after the holidays and I'll find ya some better suspects. Oops," she finished, laughing. "I meant prospects."

"I hate that winch," B.L. and Marc said together.

"What's hate got to do with anything?" I asked, concerned.

"Yeah," Stuart chimed in. "People like her are just try-ing to push your buttons. She's programming you to fail and you can't fall for it."

"Are y'all here 'cause y'all feel guilty since Thanksgiv-ing's comin'?" Marc asked, looking us over.

"We're here because we care," I answered.

"Yeah," B.L. shot back. "It seems like everybody cares around Thanksgiving and Christmas."

"Well, Thanksgiving's not that big a deal to us," Stuart told them. "When he says we care it's because we do."

"Can we cut the preaching and go to Dave and Buster's?" B.L. asked, clearly unimpressed.

"Are you allowed to go there?" I asked, looking at Marc.

"Y'all are the adults," he answered. "We can go wher-ever the hell y'all take us."

"Let's do it," Stuart said, reaching for his coat.

"That's a bet," B.L. answered, smiling and reaching to-ward his waist.

Van Whitfield

Then he did something that shocked me even more than my run-in with that nonspelling robber from last night. It was like one of those Technicolor, slow-motion moments. They happen when you're out with that dreaded "other woman" and you just happen to run into your girl's best friend. Your heart races, your throat tightens and you literally can't move. You know she's pulling out a cell phone to call your lady and that you're one step from life support. You told her you were at work late or that you were sick and that you couldn't leave the house or accept company. And as you literally watch her best friend call, you squirm and gracefully try to tell the "other woman" that the date you just started has to suddenly end. And she's not about to leave because the panic in your eyes tells her that you've just been busted and she doesn't care. She probably knew you were cheating anyway, and she's not about to give up her free meal. It's like the entire world around you slows to a snail's pace and, in an instant, you know what a stroke victim goes through. Desperation. Confusion. Fear. That's how it happens. And that's exactly how I felt.

B.L. slowly turned toward me and revealed what appeared to be a shiny, chrome 9 mm pistol. And what made it worse was turning around to find his "baby brother," Marc, extracting a shiny, black 9 mm from his waist.

"Am I missing something here?" I asked, easing toward Stuart.

"What are you guys up to?" Stuart asked, his back now up against mine.

"What the hell you think we doing?" B.L. asked, staring us down.

"What you *expect* us to do with these?" Marc asked, stepping toward me.

The moment was completely surreal. I felt like Lucille Ball when she was tied at the stake by a set of maniacal twins.

Lucy merely wanted to baby-sit, much like we wanted to be mentors. So what if our intentions weren't exactly noble? They didn't know that. Did they? We wanted to score points with the ladies. Is that so bad? As I clenched my eyes in fear, I saw Lucy, desperately trying to tear herself away from that stake. And like her, I thought, *I should start carrying a purse—it worked for Eve... God could have at least given us one last trip to Dave and Buster's... And where the hell is that loudmouth Ethel when* we *need her?*

I didn't know what would happen, how it would happen or if they'd snatch my keys and ride off into the sunset after they rubbed us out. I only wanted it to be over fast. And to my surprise, it was.

We can't take these to Dave and Buster's," B.L. told us, referring to their weapons. "They have that ride thing that turns you upside down and if these fell out," he said before pausing. "Bam!" he yelled, raising his gun, and forcing more shakes out of us than a pan of Jell-O. "It's over."

"Yeah," Marc added. "If we get jammed with these, our PO will violate us and it's goodbye parole, hello D.C. jail."

"We'll hide them in the bathroom down the hall and get them when we come back tomorrow," B.L. said, headed toward the door.

"You guys are coming back tomorrow?" Stuart asked, still obviously amazed that they had guns.

"Problee," Marc answered, removing a clip loaded with silver-plated bullets from his pocket. "Y'all will call Platz and tell her y'all want some calmer-type fools that y'all can control."

"And we'll waste another afternoon trippin' off some clowns that don't want nothin' to do with us," B.L. remarked, walking through the door. "That's how it always works."

How the hell did they expect it to work? I wondered as they headed toward the door. *You can't find a mentor when you're carrying a gun.*

I hated to admit it, but Ms. Burnout 2000 was on target. We were in over our heads and worse than that, we were in for trouble.

chapter 9

Dave and Buster's Meets Simon, Marc, Stuart, B.L. and Evelyn

Twenty Minutes Later

Simon

D ave and Buster's, which most locals called D & B's, was one of the top first-date spots in the area. It featured an awe-inspiring collection of high-tech video games, indoor golf, football and basketball challenges and simulated carnival rides. If you were going out on a blind date or a date who made you wish you were blind, D & B's was a perfect spot. First of all, the flashing lights from the midway area helped even the homeliest of women look decent. And the flip side was that it barely mattered if you were out with damaged goods, because so many other guys took their less than perfect dates to D & B's.

I just wondered how many were out with dates who had to hide their guns before they made the trek up Rockville Pike and into White Flint Mall.

O kay, fellas," Stuart said, reaching in his pocket. "You're good for ten bucks apiece."

"Ten bucks?" B.L. answered, upset.

"You gonna have to come stronger than that," Marc told him.

"Look, Stu," I said, walking toward a long, curling line. "Last time we were here we went through fifty bucks in less than an hour."

"*We* have jobs," he reminded me, glaring at B.L. and Marc.

With that little pronouncement we joined the line to purchase game cards and considered our fate. On the ride over, B.L. and Marc proved to be quite inquisitive and amazingly bright. They asked where we were from and why we decided to be mentors. Like many others, they wanted to know how we'd passed the age of twenty-five without two kids apiece, and no jail records or arrests. "What are y'all, feds or cops or narcs or something?" B.L. asked, concerned. Marc had a keen interest in books and literature and like Stuart, B.L. had a way with numbers. Of course, both of them were major wrestling fans and knew the entire life stories of each and every WWF and WCW grappler alive. What really struck me was their fas-cination with the lives of others. They were hungry for details and insatiable in their desire for more information. I imagined they'd both make credible journalists. And I also considered that their disappointment with their lives fueled their appetites.

"So, Simon," Marc said, standing beside me. "If y'all are all that, how come y'all ain't got wives or nothing?"

"I already told you, it's not our fault," I answered, my eyes searching the huge room. "We can't help it if women don't know what they want."

"I guess what you're really saying is that they don't want y'all," B.L. remarked.

"I don't think so," Stuart interrupted. "I think we're saying that it's none of your business and that if you guys don't shut your traps, we'll rise up out of here before we waste another minute."

"Wasn't nobody talkin' to you," quipped Marc. "I'm asking my main man Simon."

"It don't matter," B.L. said, quieting Marc. "If them not being able to find a wife means we get to play Cop Marauder, I don't care if they don't never get married."

Stuart and I gave each other a long, nervous look. It was clear our thoughts were engaged in a long, slow tango. Everywhere we went, it became a subject of discussion. Though getting married wasn't on Stuart's agenda, it was a topic that dominated my thoughts. *What's wrong with us ... Why don't we have wives?*

It was ridiculous. Even as we stood in line, it hit us like rabid, Hall of Fame linebacker Lawrence Taylor once slammed into nervous, life-loving quarterbacks. Why were we such losers when it came to women? The stats were in our favor. There were clearly more single women than single, available men. As we looked ahead of us in line, we couldn't help but notice couples hugging, kissing and even holding hands as we endured B.L. and Marc's insistent questions. I should have been there with Eve and I'm sure Stuart's mind raced toward Lynn. I could see that our charges weren't about to let up. And I'd been humiliated enough for one night.

I had to make a move.

"Look," I said, reaching for my wallet and grabbing a twenty. "I'm going to scope this place out and I'll meet you back here."

"Coward," Stuart said, as I walked away.

"Coward" is right, I thought as I walked away. I headed toward D & B's version of a testosterone tank, the basket-ball cage. The testosterone oozed in the basketball cage because men of every color, creed and religion went there to show what they were made of and to flex in front of their dates. The aim of the game was simple. You spent two bucks for a chance to sink three free throws into a tiny rim. And if you were lucky and somehow knocked down three shots in a row, you and your date walked away with an eighteen-cent Kewpie doll.

Most of the guys I knew sincerely believed that if they could just locate the six inches of height God meant for them to have, they'd be NBA superstars. They played ball on the weekends, shot hoops in the driveway, and had play-off and NBA draft parties to celebrate their love of basketball. The one thing that was usually missing from the equation was women. Even with the advent of the WNBA, most women could care less about the play-offs. They had no desire to hang out at draft-night parties. And they'd rather watch Emeril from the Food Channel yell "Bam!" at a plate of runny eggs than watch you clank foul shots in your driveway. But the hoops cage changed that. The woman was there, and Emeril wasn't, so she had no choice but to watch you.

A guy was in the cage warming up who I imagined was about to make a huge fool of himself. He bricked the first two shots so bad, I thought they would award him a masonry degree on the spot. And when the third one banged off the rim and flew over the twelve-foot-high fence, I said a prayer and wondered if God was too tied up to move the rims at D & B's. My prayer was short-lived and the answer came quicker than I ever expected, because when the game attendant swiped his card and started the game, he sunk the first shot like he and Michael Jordan were first cousins.

A woman was standing right behind him cheering him on and letting him know that he was the man. And for what? He still had another two shots to sink until he'd win a Kewpie doll. I gathered she knew what she was talking about when he tossed the ball toward the rim and made it two in a row. I couldn't believe it. I'd never made one shot. Much less two in a row. I didn't know why it bothered me so much, but it killed me that the guy in the cage was probably stuck in testosterone overload. There was no way he would miss the last shot. He could turn backward, throw the ball between his legs and the shot was going to drop.

Needless to say, the third shot was nothing but net and she screamed like he'd just hit the winning basket for the NBA championship. I hated it. He'd made the shots, he had a date while I didn't and worst of all, he was about to hand her a Kewpie doll. Didn't she know I would have given her a Kewpie doll? I would have bought her a stupid Kewpie doll. Hell, I would have given her anything she wanted because when it struck me that I recognized the voice, Eve was the woman who was about to get a Kewpie doll.

"Eve," I said, tapping her on the shoulder. "Is that you?"

"It depends on who you are," she said, slowly turning around. "Oh," she went on, obviously disappointed. "My name's Gail. And I hope you find your Eve."

"Hey, babe," said her date, handing her a truly hideous-looking stuffed Kewpie doll. "This is for you."

"I love it," she told him, grabbing his arm and walking away. "I never knew you were such a good ball player," she added, kissing him on the cheek.

He then gave me an obnoxious wink and said, "You should give it a shot, big fella. The ladies love it."

I now had good reason to hate him. Not only had he won a dumb Kewpie doll for his dumb date, but he had the nerve to tell me what the ladies would like after he made certain that I wasn't sporting a lady. This experience, meeting Marc and B.L. and once again being reminded of my perilous fate with women, was one I hadn't counted on. I figured I'd get heavenesque brownie points for just wanting to help some wayward kids and instead I got Mrs. Platz blowing smoke in my face *and* up my ass. And instead of two innocent wayward boys, I got two parolees with more bullets than teeth. I didn't get it. And when I spotted a familiar strut prancing around the virtual-reality golf simulator, I knew my luck was about to change.

This time, it really was Eve!

"You should keep your head down," I said as she sliced a ball into a well-placed video water hazard.

"And you should keep your mouth to yourself," she said, stomping her foot as her ball splashed in a tiny lake.

"I kept my mouth to myself last night," I reminded her. "I was hoping you wouldn't make me go that way two nights in a row."

"Simon?" she said, looking up and then searching the room like her eyes had radar. "What are you doing here?"

"Actually, me and my partner just came up this way with two kids that we mentor."

"You mentor," she said, sounding impressed. "That's great."

"We figured that," I blurted out.

"You figured what?" she asked, reaching for another club.

"We figured it would look great to women," I said, realizing that my size-twelves had just gotten a taste test in my very own mouth.

"Please don't tell me you're mentoring to score points with women, Simon," she remarked, again looking about the room. "That's not what mentoring is about."

"We know that," I said, turning to see if Stuart had noticed I'd made contact with a living, breathing woman. "We're on a give-back deal and giving back to the community is what we're about."

"Well that's certainly better than doing it to impress a woman," she said, punching numbers into the game's computer. "If you're involving yourself with kids, it's got to be real."

"Is that right?" I asked, starting to lean against the knee-level white fence that led to the game area. "Speaking of real," I went on. "How about you and me keeping it real since we're both here."

"I thought you were mentoring," she said.

"I can mentor and hang out," I said, winking at her. "I'm talented like that."

"Well, I'm not," she said, drawing back to swing at a golf ball. "Damn!" she exclaimed, as it again ended up in the water on the huge video screen. "Look, Simon," she started, looking around the room. "I'm here with someone, so hanging out isn't an option. Call me tomorrow and we'll work something out."

"You're on a date?" I asked, surprised. "How can you be on a date? We just went out last night."

"Excuse me," she said, firmly. "I date when I want to date and *who* I want to date," she reminded me. "And for the record, I'm not on a date, I'm here with a client," she added, again searching the room.

"So me, you and your client can hang," I said, trying to ease the tension that was creeping into our conversation.

"Is that right, Simon?" she asked sounding sarcastic. "And I guess your little 'mentees' will ride shotgun."

"How did you know?" I asked, thinking back to Marc and B.L.'s mini-arsenal.

"How did I know what?" she asked, setting up her next shot on the computer.

"About the guns?" I asked, shaking my head "no" when I noticed that she selected a nine iron to drive her ball out of the water hazard. With a choice that bad, her ball might as well spring gills.

"I don't know about any guns," she said, at the top of her backswing. "But I do know this," she said, slicing through her swing.

"What's that, Eve?"

"You're screwing up my game," she told me. "I'd sunk three birdies in a row until you showed up," she insisted. "So why don't you call me later and we'll get together for lunch or something with your little protégés."

"I'll hold you to that," I answered, backing away from the golf cage. "By the way," I added. "I'm not screwing up your game," I told her. "You have a terrible backswing and you're just not much of a golfer."

"And you are?" she asked, unimpressed.

"Let's put it like this," I said, proudly. "You can't use a nine iron in the water," I told her. "You need to put your driver to work."

"My driver?" she said, searching her bag.

"That's the ticket."

"So you're really into golf?" she asked.

"Check this out," I told her. "My friends think I should be on the tour," I lied. "And if you'd like to tighten up your game, I'll come on as your coach."

"You'll coach me?" she asked, excited. "On a real course?"

"After that driver puts you on the green, you'll probably call me to hit the links tomorrow morning," I bragged.

"My driver," she commented, now whispering to herself. "I could have probably saved three strokes if I had been using my driver," she said, tightening up on her grip. "Thanks, Simon," she said, nodding her head. "I've never been in the drink before, and I used my nine iron because it's the only Big Bertha in my bag," she remarked. "And don't forget, you said you'd coach me," she said, practicing a swing. "Okay, driver, do your thing, get mommy out of this water."

"I'm going to check on my fellas and then I'm heading to the bathroom," I said, turning to walk away. "When I get back, I expect to see your name on the leader board."

"You can count on it, coach," she said, giving me a thumbs-up.

As I walked away, I felt proud. She'd taken my advice and was about to stroke her ball onto the putting green. She'd saved me with the robber and I'd saved her golf game. In the grand scheme of things, as far as I was concerned, we were even.

"Damn you, Simon!" I heard her yell, as I headed toward the bathroom and back toward Marc, B.L. and Stuart. "I'm still stuck in this stupid water trap!"

chapter 10

Stuart, Simon, Lynn and the Client

Eight Seconds Later

Stuart

A driver in a water trap, Simon," I said, shaking my head in disbelief. "Are you out of your mind?"

"She just has a bad swing," he answered.

"How would you know?" I asked, turning to locate the golf cage. "You've never played golf in your life."

"What are you talking about, Stu?" Simon inquired. "I could coach *you*," he told me. "I won the U.S. Open Pro-Am on my PlayStation2 last week."

"And I've won the NBA championship on Dreamcast for three years in a row," I remarked. "But that doesn't make me Michael Jordan."

"Quit hatin', Stuart," he said, looking me in the eye. "You're just PO'd because my little hottie is in the house."

"Your little hottie is a figment of your imagination and we both know that," I reminded him. "You've known this so-called Eve forever, but as far as I know, no one has ever seen her."

"Stuart," he answered, smiling. "My imagination could *never* be that good. I'm telling you she's here. I just talked to her," he told me. "She's wearing a cute little black miniskirt and a tight red top. We can go check her out. She's playing that virtual golf game right now."

"It's Friday night and every woman in here has on a cute little black miniskirt," I remarked, looking about. "I think it's their official date uniform," I told him. "But let's see your little hottie in action, 'coach'," I said sarcastically.

"Point well taken, Stu," he acknowledged. "Check this," he said, now smiling. "She's no Tiger Woods, but I'd carry her bag any day of the week."

"You won't have to," I commented as we edged toward the golf game. "She's got a line of caddies waiting already," I said, surprised at the throng of men surrounding the cage.

"She's Tiger Woods," one guy whispered.

"That's her third birdie in a row," another remarked.

"Birdie?" his buddy answered. "She's about to eagle this hole."

"I thought you said she couldn't golf," I said, trying to catch a glimpse of Simon's "make-believe" girlfriend.

"Obviously my advice paid off," he boasted. "PlayStation2 is no different than Augusta in April," he added. "Golf is golf."

And big is big, I thought, inspecting the cage.

No wonder Simon had kept Eve out of sight. Guys had a tendency to do that with women they believed would embarrass them. Contrary to popular belief, the real testing criterion for men was the first meeting with friends. A guy who refused to introduce his lady friend to his buddies was sending a major message. Many women mistakenly believed that the family introduction is the telling barometer. Women used to constantly pester me about meeting my grandmother. They convinced themselves that an introduction to her meant they had to be special.

Little did they know.

For the average guy, a family intro was easy and relatively painless. Men knew they could show up to the family reunion with Bozo's blue-headed stepsister and no one would say a word. They'd offer her corn on the cob, a slab of ribs and some of Aunt Mildred's dreadful meat pie. She'd be invited to pose for the family picture, encouraged to sport one of those nauseating family tree T-shirts and asked who keeps her blue locks so bright and bouncy. And when you cruised through the next family reunion with an entirely different blue-haired Bozo stepsister type, no one—not your mom, dad, sister or brother—would bat an eye.

Guys knew that and it was the reason why so many women were reduced to being mere parade participants when it came to meeting family. But meeting friends was where the real test lay. Your family thought they knew your dating habits. Your friends absolutely knew your habits, particularly because they helped to shape them. No sane guy would offer up an introduction to his secret booty-call babe because, unlike family, buddies demanded explanations.

"Have you lost your mind?" one would ask.

"You can't be that pressed," another would muse.

"I know she's kind of tough on the eyes," a buddy might comment. "But does she have any single friends?"

I knew the drill, because I'd been through it before. I hated it when it happened to me and often relished the fact that I could pull off these very same lines on a dim-witted friend who dared to strut a losing lady around our buddies. But I was feeling a bit sorry for Simon. If he thought the woman smacking golf balls around the cage was a "hottie" at any level, he was even more lost than I thought he was.

"So this is Ms. Eve, the one who can't golf," I said, my head shaking in disbelief.

"Yeah," he answered, proudly. "She's got a hitch in her backswing, but we can work on that."

"That's not all you need to work on," I told him, holding in a laugh.

"What are you talking about, Stuart?"

"I'm talking about your little . . . my bad," I added, still trying not to laugh. "I mean your b-i-g hottie."

"What are you talking about?" he repeated.

"You said she was wearing a cute little black miniskirt and tight red top."

"She is," he told me.

"I guess this is one of those rare instances where 'little' is relative and 'tight' is a truly literal term."

Then he looked up and seemed nearly as shocked as I was.

"Damn," he said, his head snapping back. "That's not her, Stu."

"She's exactly like you described," I joked. "Black miniskirt and red top," I added. "I'm proud of you, Simon. I just can't wait for Rod and Trevor to meet her," I laughed. "Of course they'll have to reassess our grocery budget for the Cancun trip, but after last year, maybe they've already built it in."

"Look, Stu," he said, sounding worried. "She's not Eve. Eve is like a size six, not a sixteen."

"And last time I checked, you're a vehicle operator and not a bus driver," I reminded him. "Your delusions of grandeur never cease to amaze me," I told him. "But I have to admit, your Eve there—she's pretty grand."

Even he had to laugh, because in the cage was a woman who out-sized Simon and he carried quite a load all his own. As Simon had always told us, Eve was as cute as they come. But she was nowhere near a size six. And if I were a betting man, I'd say the only time she'd ever seen a size six was the day she was born.

"I'm telling you that's not her," Simon insisted.

"I'd be telling me that's not her too," I answered, laughing.

"C'mon, Stu," he pleaded. "You know she's not my type," he told me. "And besides, Eve's backswing could never match hers."

"And I guess her back-*side* doesn't match hers either," I answered.

"Don't think that I'm just trying to change the topic," he said, looking around. "But where are the boys?"

"They already told you about that boy stuff," I reminded him.

"Well, since the *boys* aren't around, I'll call it like I see it."

"I gave them their game cards so they're probably somewhere around here wrecking havoc on some poor, unsuspecting machine," I said, turning back to watch the woman in the golf cage.

"Look, Stu," Simon started, tapping me on the shoulder. "I'm going to see if I can track them down."

"Cool," I said, amazed at a hole-in-one scored by the golf-club-wielding amazon everyone was watching. "I'll stay here and keep an eye on your *Ms. Eve.*"

"I already told you that's not her," he warned.

"Well, maybe I'll run into Lynn," I said, laughing. "In fact," I added, "maybe she'll play golf next, and I'll flag you down so you can give her lessons too."

Then I considered it. Lynn wouldn't be caught dead in a place like D & B's. She had that whole classy thing going. I couldn't imagine that she'd be into video games, much less golf. Golf would be way too boring for her. She liked excitement. Bright lights, brightly colored "girlie" drinks and big, booming bass speakers move her. She'd never stand for fun and games that lead to nothing. Except when it came to our relationship. That was more fun and games than I'd ever endured in my life. And it led to absolutely nothing.

But seeing her the night before made me realize how much fun she could be. All day long, I'd thought of hanging out with her on the trip. I wouldn't think twice about the screwed-up water in Mexico if she came along. And I knew she'd come, especially since she thought I looked like Denzel. I hated thinking about a woman this much. But I couldn't help it. Anytime a woman said you even faintly resembled someone like Denzel, she got inside your head.

And Lynn had gotten so deep inside my head that I could swear she'd just walked by me.

*Y*ou *must be more pressed than a pair of prison slacks*, I thought, worried. A quick refocus all but confirmed it. That sassy strut. Those beautiful legs. And the alluring essence of Fendi's Theorema cologne hanging in the air. Nobody could run that combination together and not be her. And if it wasn't her, I was willing to make a fool of myself to find out. I hurried to catch her and then slowed to a cool, steady pace when she approached a white-water-rafting game. My mind raced for a smooth entry line. One that would speak to my surprise at seeing her, while not giving away the fact that I'd spent the greater part of the day completely mesmerized with thoughts about her.

"Hello, miss," I said, approaching her from behind.

"Stuart," she casually replied. "What are you doing here?"

"How did you know it was me?" I asked, surprised.

"I saw you following me," she said, turning around.

"I wasn't following you."

"If you weren't following me, why did you try to hide behind the snowboarding machine when I turned around?" she asked.

"It wasn't a snowboarding machine and I wasn't hiding," I answered, smiling. "It was a skateboarding game and I thought I'd give it a try," I told her. "And if you don't mind me asking," I finished, "what are *you* doing here?"

"I'm here with an associate," she answered. "We do some work together," she told me. "I've known him for years."

"Is your 'associate' one of those jealous types who'll lose his cool if he sees you talking to a debonair man like my-self?" I asked, straightening my lapels.

"I think not," she replied, shaking her head "no."

"So where is he?" I inquired.

"Who knows?" she casually asked. "I'm not looking for him, are you?"

"Not really," I said, thinking of Simon's description of Eve. Lynn was wearing a "date uniform" too. She had on a sharp little miniskirt, but there was no tight red top, as he'd described. She was wearing a neatly zipped, thin black waist-jacket.

"You want to play?" she asked, sitting on the machine.

"I'm not much for games," I told her.

"Why would someone who's not into games come here?" she asked. "This is game city U.S.A."

"Maybe I *was* just following you," I answered, trying to get in *her* head, like she'd often tried with me.

"If you were following me, you'd know I'm into games in a major way," she remarked. "Don't you remember our relationship?" she asked, smiling.

"How could I forget? You played me better than my buddy plays PlayStation2."

"You played yourself," she commented, now sitting at the game.

"That may have been the case," I told her. "But we can change all of that right now."

"So let's change it," she said, looking me dead in the eye. "We can start with a game."

"Are you saying you want to play me in a game?" I asked, taken aback. "Is this a challenge?"

"I don't consider it a challenge," she answered, starting to stand. "You name the game and I'll beat you like nobody's business."

"And what do I get when I beat you?" I asked, sizing her up.

"Remember last night when you started to mention something with your friends?" she asked. "Beat me in golf, and we'll make it happen."

"I'll make it easy on you," I said, smiling. "Pick your favorite game and I'll beat you so bad you'll think my name is Stuart Sega instead of Stuart Worthington."

"Okay, Mr. Sega," she remarked, reaching for my hand. "Why don't we play a little game called golf."

"You play golf?" I asked, surprised.

"Like a champ," she answered.

"Golf it is," I replied, reaching for her hand. "I have a buddy who's really into golf," I confessed. "Since you're a champ, I'm sure you won't mind if he coaches me."

"Who needs a coach?" she shot back. "We can get this thing done right now."

I need a coach, I thought, worried.

But, she was right. It was about to get done. I wasn't going to lose to *any* woman. Even one as tight as Lynn. Who cares if I'd never played golf in my life? My only hope was that Simon would get back from the bathroom before we really got started.

I also hoped that his "amazon Eve," who had been tearing up the course moments earlier, hadn't heard everything I'd said about her. Because if she hadn't, it wouldn't

Van Whitfield

seem so bad when I begged Simon to ask her to help me beat Lynn.

When you were playing for all the marbles, you had to pull out all the stops. Even if one of the stops doubled you in weight and size.

And even if that stop was a woman.

The Coach, the Boys, the Client and the Bathroom

Sixteen Seconds Later

Simon

t was official. Stuart was a nut. How could he have let two gun-toting desperados like Marc and B.L. loose in a wide-open spot like D & B's? It was obvious that they had the ability to turn the place upside-down in a matter of minutes. They weren't the type to just walk around and appreciate all that D & B's had to offer. The bells and whistles and the myriad of super-high-tech video monitors and midway-style games of chance wouldn't be enough to hold their attention. Especially on ten dollars. They needed r-e-a-l money to have a good time. And unlike most every grown man here, our "boys" were the types who would pursue that money Malcolm X–style—by any means necessary.

I'd spent the last ten minutes treating D & B's like a Thomas' English muffin. I'd been through every nook and cranny. And no luck. Marc and B.L. were nowhere to be found. My thoughts swayed between locating Eve to prove to Stuart that I wasn't a total whack job and calling 911 to alert the world that a two-man crime wave had been unleashed within the confines of comfy, secure White Flint Mall. Though the 911 call was an option I felt I owed to my fellow man, there was no way I could pull it off.

Ultimately, a call like that would land me and Stuart on TV. We'd have to explain how we'd allowed two young toughs like Marc and B.L. out of our sight. Then we'd have to divulge our knowledge of their guns and admit that we had no idea as to where they'd hidden their ammo. But worst of all, we'd have to confess that we'd escorted them to D & B's for a friendly, Friday evening outing, and given them just ten dollars apiece to play games and entertain themselves. Some would consider that abusive. And the single women we were trying to impress would consider us cheap.

And the only thing worse than an abusive man, is an abusive man who's cheap.

I headed to the bathroom and figured I could gather myself there. I guessed that Marc and B.L. were probably walking about the mall, staking it out and planning a "details at eleven" type holdup. Stuart and I had managed to fail royally. We failed our mentees, failed Mrs. Platz and in a strange kind of way, we failed ourselves. Eve was right.

We were mentoring for the wrong reason. There had to be a better way to impress a woman. We'd already tried the traditional route. We had money in the bank. Stuart had a better wardrobe than any woman we knew. We had nice rides. Nice houses. And did I mention, we had money in the bank? That alone is usually enough to impress a woman. But in our case, it didn't seem to matter.

We rarely got to the point where our bankrolls made a difference. Women were usually long gone by then. I remember one date where I literally left my checkbook on the console in my Range Rover. I stopped at a 7-Eleven, in hopes that she would check my balance. I opened it. Shook it in her face. And walked into the store knowing she would do the typical woman thing and sneak a peek. Sadly, it didn't work. She fell for the bait just as I suspected. But she was clumsy.

My checkbook ended up stuck in a narrow crevice that separated the console from the seat. I couldn't dare acknowledge that I'd left my checkbook out on purpose anymore than she could squeal that she'd dropped it. So we rode the streets of D.C. in complete silence wondering which of us was really the bad guy. My only advantage was that she hadn't clipped me for any checks and that a carwash attendant located it a week later.

Sadly, he managed to clip me for a check before I handed over a tiny reward.

As I considered it, I realized that we'd never reap the rewards of working with Marc and B.L. They were time enough for us and just about anyone else I knew. And when I heard their raspy, yet still-young voices leap from a handicap stall in the bathroom, I knew the worst was yet to come.

"C'mon, Marc!" B.L. exclaimed. "You can do it!"

"What if I do it wrong?" Marc answered, worried.

I couldn't believe it. Our little pistol-packing mentee was all of ten years old and he couldn't use the bathroom on his own. I'd read about this before. Kids who'd been deprived of a male role model, who'd made it to advanced ages without regard for basic grooming and bathroom habits. These were kids who'd been brought up on the fringes. They needed patience, concern and understanding. They deserved better than what Stuart and I were offering. My desire to mentor them changed on the spot. I wanted the best for them and knew they deserved the best I had to offer.

Unfortunately, they also seemed interested in the best that someone else had to offer.

"Get it right this time, kid," a considerably older voice boomed. "It's time for you to be a man."

Oh my God, I thought, worried. *B.L. can't be pimping out his own little brother.*

"Just close your eyes," B.L. begged. "It'll be over before you know it."

"But what if we get caught?" Marc asked, his voice sounding strained.

"If you hurry up and get it over with you won't get caught," the older voice replied.

That was all I needed to hear. I wasn't about to let B.L. force Marc into anything. Even if my pants were unzipped. I raced toward the stall and rushed to push it open. But as the door swung open, it was clear I was too late. B.L.'s glance rushed toward me and then to the older gentleman. I was in shock at the scene before me. And I'm sure they were in shock at what they were seeing as well.

I just didn't know if they were more shocked with the fact that my pants were resting casually around my ankles or whether they were repulsed by the fact that I was wearing a pair of bright red, skintight, spaghetti-string bikini briefs with a huge yellow Pokémon cartoon character etched across the front.

"Damn," B.L. said, laughing hysterically. "Did those come with a matching top?"

"No wonder you can't find no wife," Marc commented, slapping his brother five.

"You cheated me, you little cocksucker," the older man said, turning around. "Simon?" he then asked, surprised. "What are you doing in here?"

"Vic?" I asked, shocked at the sight of my favorite strip-club owner. "What the hell are you doing in here?"

"Yo, Simon, you know him?" B.L. asked.

"Do you know these little cheats?" Vic asked, starting to stand.

"Do I know them?" I asked, upset. "I'm their mentor," I asserted, crossing my arms. "And I'm shocked that you're in here with them, Vic," I told him. "You could have any woman you want," I added. "I never even knew you went this way," I said, shaking my head. "And with two kids, Vic," I went on. "I'm just glad I got here before you went too far."

"Speaking of which," Vic said, smiling. "Are you happy to see me or is that one of them there Pokémon things in your shorts?"

"Damn, Simon," B.L. said, laughing. "I bet it's Pikachu."

I felt like a complete grade-A jerk. Here I was, proclaiming my virtues as a man and a mentor and I was standing in a bathroom stall with my pants hugging my ankles and they thought I had a hard-on? Didn't they know that guys who wore their underwear too small looked like they were packing? It's just like a woman who tries to stuff her B-cups into an A-cup bra. She looks bigger than she really is. I'd done it with my underwear for years. I just never planned on anyone seeing me in my Pokémon underwear.

As I started to pull my pants up and gather the last bit of dignity I could muster, the sound of an electric motor drew near. Someone pushed on the door and poked his head in. When I saw it was a guy in a wheelchair, I was so startled that I unknowingly lost hold of my pants. Needless to say, my embarrassment took on a whole new level.

"Dude," he said, staring at me. "You're kind of old for the Pokémon thing," he remarked. "Or is that why you're in here with the kids?"

"I'm their mentor," I told him.

"Let me guess," he said, whipping his wheelchair around. "You and the old guy here met them in an Internet chat room. I've heard about your types."

"Excuse me, sir," Vic said, lightly brushing the front of his suit. "But this isn't what it looks like. In fact, you might like some of this action."

"Yeah, right," the wheelchair-bound guy answered. "You have chubby here prancing around like some nut from that 'Real Sex' show on HBO," he added, starting to roll away. "And you, pops, I can't imagine your deal. But I gotta admit. The flower on the lapel and the little diamond tiepin," he continued. "Nice touch. I never imagined you pedophile types were into the detail thing."

"Pedophile?!" Marc angrily exclaimed. "Why is he calling us pets?!"

"He wasn't calling you pets—he was calling you cheats," Vic said, reaching for Marc's hand. "I know those dice are loaded."

"They wasn't loaded," B.L. insisted. "They was just rigged a little."

"If they were rigged," Vic remarked, staring toward them. "I want my three large back."

"You lost three hundred dollars to two kids, Vic?" I asked, surprised.

"Try three grand," he shot back. "I'm here with my stockbroker, Evelyn," he told me. "She says this place would make a great investment, but the only thing I've invested in is these frickin' kids," he bemoaned. "And these are hardly kids, I tell you. They're first-rate cheats."

"You're here with Eve?" I asked, shocked. "Well, I guess she'd be really happy to know you're playing craps with a kid who's barely ten and that you're calling *him* a cheat."

"I don't know who's cheating who," said a voice I didn't recognize. "But let's get those hands up high in the air."

I didn't even bother to turn around. Maybe it struck me that some wily armed robber overheard us and realized a ten-year-old was holding Vic's three large. And maybe the wheelchair guy alerted some cop that a far too interesting foursome was taking place in *his* bathroom stall, and that none of the participants was visibly handicapped, which made the act even more vile. And just maybe, I didn't want whoever was behind us to see the front of my cartoon-character-etched underwear. None of the options was particularly appealing. My nervous arms were as shaky as my mind. And I'm certain the burn in my eyes which resulted from the sweat that rapidly formed on my brow made me look especially uncomfortable.

But I knew sweaty brows and burning eyes had nothing to do with it. It was my damn underwear. They were way too tight. And for the moment, it appeared "tight" all but defined the moment. Me, with my pants around my ankles. Vic, who looked like a classic, old-school mobster. And two underage juveniles with a fistful of dollars. We weren't just in trouble. We were a Jerry Springer episode. And besides wishing that my pants would somehow magically rise and find a happy home around my abundant waistline, just one thing dominated my thoughts.

Pokémon sucks.

chapter 12

The Cop and His Buddy Meet the Sneezer and Big Pussy

Nine Seconds Later

Stuart

Simon had this uncanny way of letting me down. All I needed was a little coaching. It didn't matter that I'd never before picked up a golf club. I wasn't supposed to lose to a woman.

At anything!

I gather that I made a complete fool of myself when I selected *a putter* to hit my ball off the first tee. Lynn, being the good sport that she was, didn't even laugh. But when I made the tragic mistake of again picking that very same putter to take me off of the second tee, she couldn't hold it in. She laughed like Chris Rock was in the cage with us. And when the video monitor flashed Please Contact a Technician for Assistance on my third tee shot, I thought she'd land on her side. She won the first nine holes without my even sinking a single putt. I was ten-over on every hole. And though I had no clue as to what ten-over meant, I knew I was losing desperately. All she needed was one more hole and she'd be an easy winner.

And all I needed was a way out of this charade that would help me save face. I needed something quick. Something big. And something that would border on the absurd.

"Yo, Stuart," said Marc, banging on the fence. "They got your boy and he's wearing Pokémon bikinis."

"Marc?" I asked, turning around. "What are you talking about?"

"They got him in the bathroom and he had his pants down and he knew the guy he got caught with and I told them my dad could straighten the whole thing out," he belted out in rapid succession.

"You never told me you had a son, Stuart," Lynn said, surprised.

"He never told me either," I answered.

"Are you gonna come get him?" Marc asked, his voice cracking.

"I'm right behind you," I reassured him. "Look, hon," I said, handing Lynn my putter. "You got a break here," I added. "I let you win those first holes because I wanted to up the ante," I continued. "I figured you'd fall for it and promise me a date this weekend, and it almost worked," I lied. "We'll finish this up some other time," I commented, reaching for the fenced door. "I'll call you. And by the way," I finished, "you need to work on your backswing."

What a completely perfect out. Marc was beyond quick. Simon was beyond big. And the mere thought of him in Pokémon underwear was beyond absurd. I was in gold medal–level excuse territory. Lynn didn't get to finish her execution. And since my "coach" never showed, I could always blame it on that. But did I really want a coach who wears Pokémon drawers? And what the hell is Simon doing in bikinis anyway?

All of this raced through my mind as we headed to what Marc identified as the "security office."

"What's going on here, officer?" I asked, as we walked in.

"Take your pick," he answered, in a deliberate Southern drawl. "Your juvies and your perp here—"

"Perp?" I asked.

"Yeah," he said, shuffling papers. "Your perperator—"

"Excuse me," I interrupted. "What exactly do you mean when you say perpe-*rator*?"

"The perp," he answered, trying miserably to tuck his T-shirt over his ponderous belly. "Any old ways, he and Mister Lou—"

"I'll have you know my name is Victor A. D'mazio, officer," some old, white-haired guy spat out.

"Like I was sayin'," the officer continued. "Your perp and the geezer there—"

"I'm no geezer, you lummox," the old guy barked.

"Why did he call him a sneezer?" Marc asked innocently.

"He said 'geezer' and it's a guy who's gonna have us all

thrown in the slammer if he don't shut up," B.L. whispered.

"I heard you, you little cheat," the old guy whispered back. "And if you don't give me my three large back, I'll—"

"You won't do a dag-on thing there, pops," the officer told him. "You and your perp buddy here have enough explaining to do already."

"Can I talk with you about the perpetrator?" I asked, leading him away from the group.

"Perpe-*trator*?" he asked, sounding confused.

"How silly of me," I gushed. "I meant perpe-*rator*."

"Oh yeah," he said, reaching for a doughnut. "The perp," he added. "That's real police officer–type talk, you know."

Amazingly, I could hear the "perperator" and the old guy going at it while we headed down the hall.

"Are you trying to get us sent to Sing-Sing, Vic?" Simon asked, upset.

"The only thing I'm trying to do is get my money back from these midget hustlers," he replied.

"I'm not no midget, you geezer," B.L. quipped.

"Why do you keep calling him a sneezer?" Marc again asked.

It was all I could do to focus the officer on our conversation. Between his doughnut, the juvies, the perp, and the "sneezer," I had my hands full.

"Look, my friend," I told him. "These guys were probably just horseplaying," I confided, without knowing what they'd actually done. "We don't want any trouble."

"They got plenty of trouble coming," he answered. "I

caught 'em red-handed. The perp was reaching to pull his pants back up and the geezer wanted his money back 'cause they hadn't gotten to him yet."

"I'm not a geezer!" the old guy yelled from the room. "Tell him I'm not a geezer," he begged, his voice trailing off.

"This handicapped fella said they confessed the whole thing to him and they even tried to get him to join in," he told me. "The police is already on the way to haul them in. If this thing shakes out, I'm probably gonna get a promotion and I might even land a spot on 'Cops.' "

"Listen to me," I said, looking over his shoulder, and picking up the pace. "The word on the streets is that 'Cops' is on its last leg. It's about to get cancelled."

"What are you talking about?"

"You want to get on the hottest show on television?" I asked, making sure no other officers were milling about the room.

"You mean 'WWF Smackdown'?" he asked, excited.

"Even hotter than that," I whispered, knowing he was prime for my bait. "I'm talking cable. HBO. R-e-a-l hot."

"Get out," he said, standing back. "You talkin' that documentree *Pimps Up, Ho's Down*?"

"What the hell is *Pimps Up, Ho's Down*?" I asked, concerned.

"You said hot," he told me. "You said HBO," he added. "That's *gotta* be them pimps and them there ho's," he went on. "I gotta tell you," he confessed. "I kinda like some of them ho's."

"Look, buddy," I went on. "By the way, what did you say your name was?"

"Buddy."

"No. I was just calling you buddy. But I was asking you your name."

"That's what I just said," he answered. "My name is Buddy."

"Well check this out, Buddy," I said, turning him toward the old guy. "You see him?"

"You talkin' about the geezer?" he asked.

"Quit calling me geezer!" the old guy yelled.

"You recognize him?" I asked.

"Course I recognize him. He's the geezer!" Buddy exclaimed.

"Why is everybody calling him a sneezer?" Marc asked.

"Ever see 'The Sopranos'?" I quickly added.

"What are you sayin'?" he asked, focusing in on the "geezer."

"He's one of the stars and he's a very generous man," I told him. "And if we walk out of here, I'm sure he'll remember you."

"I hear those fellas are loyal like that," he said, his head nodding. "Hey, I bet you're one of them there producers," he remarked. "That's probably why you have on those fancy duds."

"Truth be told, they were probably rehearsing a scene," I whispered. "He could have you written in, you know," I went on. "You think they'll give you some time off to take some acting lessons and to tape the show?"

"I'll take the time," he answered, excited. "Hey," he said, smiling, "You think I'm good for a picture?"

"Why don't we save that for the set?" I told him.

"Good idea," he answered. "I should have thought of that."

"So, Buddy," I said, slapping him on the back. "I have

your name, I know where to reach you and I think we should get these guys out of here before the police show up," I remarked. "We don't want this to get too sticky and blow your chance to get on the show."

"You're right," he said, reaching for a set of keys. "You'se guys," he added, winking at me and laying it on thick. "He made me an offer I couldn't refuse," he told them, showing them to the back door. "We'll just chalk this up as a little misunderstanding. On behalf of D & B's, I apologize for the inconvenience."

"Cool," B.L. replied.

"I guess this means we get to keep the sneezer's money," Marc commented, bopping out.

"As soon as we hit the truck, you have to tell me how you pulled this off," Simon remarked, impressed.

"This isn't over," the old guy pronounced.

"Hey," Buddy said, tapping "The Sopranos" star on the shoulder. "Fa'get-about-it!"

"What the hell is your problem?" the old guy asked.

"Okay, okay. I'm even better at this one," our officer friend added, smiling. "Whass' u-p-p-p?!" he belted out, sounding the refrain of those hilarious super-soul-brother Bud Light commercials.

"You're a nut," Vic told him.

"And I like your style too," Buddy answered, closing the door behind him. "I'll just need you to sign this here release form," he told me.

"What's the deal, Buddy?" a real uniformed, gun-carrying police officer asked, walking through the front door. "You called about a fat perp in some Pokémon bikinis?"

"Cancel it, Marlon," Buddy answered. "Some crazy fella in a wheelchair had the story all wrong."

"I figured that," the cop replied, reaching for a dough-nut. "Fat guys and bikinis don't mix," he added, laughing. "It's not what you call your fashion statement," he told him.

"But check this out," Buddy said, excited. "Guess who was just in here?"

"Who's that, Buddy?" his colleague, Marlon, asked.

"Think about 'The Sopranos,' " he begged.

"What about 'em?" the real cop asked.

"I'm gonna be on," Buddy bragged. "They want to make me a big star and all," he said convincingly. "I'm even gonna have my own dressing room and they're talkin' about a star out there in Hollywood."

"You're telling me one of the Sopranos was here?"

"One of the stars just left," Buddy told him. "He's gonna put me in the show."

"Which one?" Marlon asked, excited. "Was it Stevie Van Zandt?"

"Bigger," Buddy remarked.

"Tony?"

"Even bigger than him."

"You can't get bigger than Tony. He's *the* star," Marlon reminded him.

"This guy is big, big," Buddy said, smiling broadly.

"Get outta here," the real cop answered, biting into his doughnut. "Hell no. It couldn't have been—"

"You got it, Marlon!" gushed Buddy.

"Big Pussy!" they yelled together.

"Hey, Buddy," Marlon asked, excited. "What did you do? What did you say to him?"

"You know exactly what I said," Buddy explained. "You ready?"

"This is what you're gonna do on the show isn't it,

Buddy?" he answered. "I love it when you do this," he admitted. "C'mon," Marlon added. "Hit me with it."

"Whass u-p-p-p-p?!" Buddy blathered.

"Whass u-p-p-p-p?!" Marlon loudly replied.

Then they turned toward me. I looked at Buddy and then at Marlon, who was staring at me behind the glaze of his darker-than-dark aviator shades. I didn't want anymore trouble. My reflexes kicked in and though I wanted no part of it, my mouth knew exactly what my brain was sending down.

"Oh," I said, gathering myself. "My bad," I told them. "Whass u-p-p-p?!" I exclaimed.

"Whass u-p-p-p?!" they replied in kind.

"You the man," Marlon commented, turning to walk away. "Buddy's gonna be a Soprano," he added, talking to himself.

"This here is one the producers," Buddy said, referring to me.

"I think I should sign that release form right about now," I whispered.

"You from Hollywood?" Marlon asked, turning around.

"You could say that," I answered, worried.

"Show me some ID," he insisted.

"ID?" I replied, concerned.

"You got a license or some producers card?"

"Producers card?" I considered. "I don't think they give us producers cards," I confessed. "But I'll go check and let's say that me and Big Pussy meet you on the westside parking lot."

"Your limo is parked here at the mall?" Marlon asked. "I didn't see any limo."

"You didn't?" I asked, concerned. "I mean, of course you didn't. It just pulled up and I need to run," I said, scribbling on the form. "You know how impatient limo drivers can be."

"If that's the case, you can ride with me," Marlon told me. "I'm on the east lot, and I'll zip you right over there."

"I wouldn't want to put you out, friend," I said, stepping toward the door. "See you in Hollywood, Buddy," I added. "Don't forget those acting lessons."

"Hey, my man!" Marlon yelled, excitedly. "I'll meet you and Big Pussy on the west side!"

"West side!" Buddy exclaimed, sounding the part of a doped-up, L.A. gang-banger.

The cop wants to meet a "goodfella," I thought, concerned. Who cares about Big Pussy? We're about to be in big trouble.

Simon's Range Rover was parked on the east lot. The very same east lot as Marlon. We could probably wait and try to sneak out behind him, but what kind of example would that set for B.L. and Marc? We were *supposed* to be setting an example. I could hear it now.

"Keep your heads down kids," I'd whisper nervously. *"If we're going to make it out of here, we have to duck the cops."*

"Why?" Marc would inevitably ask.

"Because we're the worst mentors on the planet and because the cop wants to meet Big Pussy," I'd say, shoving his head below the line of parked cars.

"I know Simon's fat," B.L. would joke, giggling, *"but how's the cop know he has a big pussy?!"*

And then we'd get caught and hauled off to jail for impersonating a TV mobster who was last seen "swimming with the fishes." The whole thing made me sick. But as I considered my evening, one that afforded me new and interesting insights in regards to the term "loser," sneaking past a starstruck cop didn't seem so bad. Mrs. Platz, the human chimney who stuck us with B.L. and Marc, all but called me a *loser*. Then Simon ran off and left me with our juvenile charges because even they realized we were *losers* because we were so thoroughly unattached. And worst of all, Lynn annihilated me in golf, thus securing me a front-and-center spot in the *losers* hall of shame.

Almost losing to Lynn is as bad as losing her, I thought as I caught up to the group and guided them toward the parking lot.

But not losing kept me on track for the trip. And that's all that really mattered.

If we could just beat Marlon to the truck and get the kids back to the receiving home, this night wouldn't have been a total loss.

I learned that I should avoid golf at all costs.

I confirmed that I had no tolerance for kids.

And I finally got a glimpse of Simon's sweetheart, Eve.

Which made me wonder... *Was he wearing the Pokémon bikinis for her?*

The 60-Day Rule

Weeks 5-6

The Prozac Period

Boy do I remember! Me and Grace in the back seat of her old man's clunky Buick, and I was about to strike gold. But she said that if we did "it," she expected a proposal. I knew that wasn't about to happen, so I pretty much gave up. She pulled me back on top of her anyway, and we were off to the races. A half a minute later, as we hurried to dress, she shocked me. "Will you marry me, Rod?" she asked, strapping on her bra. What had just happened? I couldn't let a thirty-second blast of bliss change the rest of my life. I remember saying, "No way!" but it didn't seem to matter. Grace was a woman on a mission. We did it again the next night. A week later, she had me out looking for rings. The stress. The doubt. The anxiety. I was a mess. And to this day I can't help but wonder. . . . Would we have ever gotten married if her father had had a two-seater?

Roderick Anthony Marshall
The Married Marine

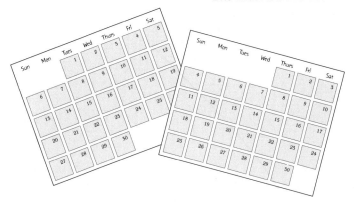

chapter 13

The Association
and the Emergency

Two Weeks Later—December 2, 2000

Simon

t'd been a fat two weeks and I hadn't seen or heard from Eve. Stuart and I had spent Thanksgiving at Rod's place. We were once more without dates and were severely out of place. Being stuck without a date on Thanksgiving usually didn't bother me, but I left D & B's thinking Eve and I had connected—we could have and perhaps even *should have* spent the holiday together. Stuart claimed he scored points with Lynn the very same night. The odds of us running into both of them on the same night in the same place were probably off the chart. But

D & B's was a popular place, so it didn't really seem so unusual.

Marc and B.L. actually thanked us for the night out and said that hanging out with Big Pussy from "The Sopranos" would give them bragging rights around the receiving home. They asked if we'd pick them up for Thanksgiving, but Stuart quickly nixed it. And when they said, "Bye y'all," when we left, I thought *I'd* cry an avalanche of tears. They stood in the doorway and stared at us until my SUV became a part of the night. Something tells me we could drive past that cruddy, run-down shack of a home right now and they'd still be standing on the porch waiting for us to come back and turn the nightmare that was their lives into a dream.

But Stuart wouldn't let that happen. He made it clear as he checked the passenger-side mirror and we raced back into Maryland. "Old lady Platz was on the money," he told me. "I don't ever want to see those fools again."

"They're not so bad," I replied, starting to merge onto D.C.'s main thoroughfare, New York Avenue. "At least they were honest."

"And we weren't?" he asked, surprised.

"We went in for all the wrong reasons," I stated. "Even Eve peeped us on that."

"Eve should mind her business and find a diet," he remarked, laughing.

I knew setting Stuart straight was useless. As far as he was concerned, the supersized woman he'd spotted in the golf cage was Eve. And I was certain he'd let me know about it each and every chance he got.

"Hey, Rod and Trevor, you should have seen Ms. Eve,"

Stuart joked when we got to Rod's place. "If you put her and Simon together they could start a reunion tour for Two Tons of Fun."

"That would probably be better than Diana Ross and her 'I'm not really trying to have a reunion' tour," Rod laughed sarcastically.

"Can you believe her?" Trevor asked. "She got eighteen million and only wanted to give Mary Wilson three."

"I wouldn't have given Mary Wilson *two* mil," Stuart huffed. "When I close my eyes and hear 'Baby Love,' I'm not seeing anybody's Mary Wilson."

"Check it," I said, jumping in. "Mary's okay, but she wasn't the one floating the Supremes' boat."

"And that, my friends, comes from a man who has an inside line on boats and other flotation devices," Stuart said, raising a drink. "The woman he's bringing on the trip probably has her own port."

"Give it a break, Stu," I begged. "I told you that wasn't Eve."

"Who wasn't Eve?" Rod immediately asked.

"Our boy Simon is all hooked up with his twin," Stuart remarked, grinning. "She's a big-boned baby with a hell of a golf game."

"When did you start playing golf?" Trevor asked, reaching for a chair.

"We were at D & B's and Stuart believes this woman who was hacking away in the golf cage is Eve," I told them. "But it wasn't her, so that's that. Let's drop it."

"Agreed," Trevor said, rubbing his hands. "Look, fellas," he started. "Rod and I have a bit of a proposition."

"I propose that you and Rod kiss my ass," Stuart interrupted. "I know where this is going and I'm not trying to go there."

"First of all, I'm not about to kiss up on nobody's ass," Rod said, sounding agitated. "And second, why don't you sit your frail ass back and listen before you run off at the mouth."

I knew Stuart would take Rod's counsel. Rod could bark out orders like he was still an active-duty marine drill sergeant. And when he dared raised his voice, or said anything with even the slightest edge, people listened. At thirty, he was still imposing in stature—his barrel chest, expansive shoulders and massive arms might as well have been a twenty-four-hour infomercial for strength, fortitude and fitness. And his gravelly, bass-heavy vocal chords would give Barry White a run for his money.

"I'm feeling you, dude," Stuart said, retreating. "That was a relative 'kiss my ass.' I didn't mean it in the literal sense."

"I guess that makes you a wimp," I commented, smiling. "And I mean wimp in a relative sense, of course," I told him.

"Why don't you kiss this wimp's ass?" Stuart shot back.

"Do you mean figuratively or literally?" Trevor asked, cracking open a Sprite.

"Figuratively," Stuart answered, smiling. "And when he's done, you and that airhead wife of yours can kiss it too," he added, staring at Trevor. "And just so we all understand each other here, I mean y'all can kiss my ass in a completely literal sense."

"Drop it, Stu," Rod commanded tersely. "Leave Leigh out of this."

"I only put her in it in a figurative sense, so consider her out of it, big fella," Stuart answered.

Rod seemed tense, which meant we were in for something important. In nearly thirty years of knowing him, I'd seen Rod get upset exactly twice. Once was at his twenty-sixth birthday surprise party. We thought he was pissed because he didn't care for the element of surprise and the embarrassment that can come with it. We soon learned he was mad because he couldn't dance and he felt that was a weakness. He still refused to acknowledge any weaknesses. The other time was when a car salesman paid a little too much attention to Grace. She'd purchased a used Volvo and the guy generously offered her a lifetime grease and lube job. Of course, Rod didn't take a liking to his offer. Especially when the sales rep said to Grace; "I have the best grease rack in D.C. and all of my customers come back for my special lube jobs."

After Rod got to him, I don't think his "grease rack" ever made it out of D.C. General Hospital.

Rod fully understood and appreciated how his size alone intimidated even the very best of his friends. Maintaining his composure and his shell of invincibility was as important to him as his family's well-being. He didn't yell, didn't complain and firmly believed in making the most of just about any circumstance. He once walked in on his twins, Koko and Loko, engaged in a truly compromising four-way encounter in their bedroom with two of his next-door neighbor's sons. Instead of yelling at the "interlopers," as he called them, he told us he sat them down, spoke in an almost cordial manner and then calmly escorted them to the door.

The next day, the poor kids' parents planted a For Sale sign in their front yard.

He never shared what he said or exactly what form of threat he issued. And that was the beauty of Rod. He had the whole "wait till your father gets home" routine down pat. Most of the dads I knew managed to keep their cool a good 99 percent of the time. But that 1 percent where they lost it is what we all feared. When that small percentage reared its ugly head, your fear forced you to believe that your father's footsteps approaching from down the hall more closely resembled those of the giant from "Jack and the Beanstalk" when he was trying to track down his golden-egg-laying goose. And when he raised his voice to make a point, you foolishly convinced yourself that dear old Dad had somehow managed to get ahold of the booming PA system from New York's Yankee Stadium. Worse yet was the moment he hit you with the classic "this is going to hurt me more than it's going to hurt you" speech. I don't know how many times I heard that as a kid, but while my father was sipping on a Bud, "agonizing in pain" and flipping channels with the remote after he'd worn me out, I was creatively attempting to soak my tender bottom in a warm tub of water, even though I was so sore I wouldn't dare sit down.

Rod was usually as laid-back as they come, but I imagine his daughters spent many an evening soaking their fannies in the family tub. I just hoped whatever was bugging him wouldn't land me and Stuart in that same tub.

"Ease up, Rod," I said, starting to stand. "You know they can't get a conversation started without Stuart going after Leigh."

"Do you have anything to do with this?" Rod said sternly, before turning toward me.

Van Whitfield

"It's okay, buddy," Trevor said, trying to calm him down. "We both know Stuart is severely limited, which is of course, why we're here."

"Yeah," Stuart said, nodding his head. "Why are we here anyway?"

"If you shut up and listen, maybe you'll find out," Rod stressed.

"We're all ears," I told him.

"Fellas," Trevor said, turning his chair around and leaning his torso against the front of the chair. "Rod and I have decided to advance your search for dates for the trip."

"No you haven't," Stuart answered. "We don't need your help, won't take it and last time I checked, we definitely didn't ask for anybody's help."

"Ditto for me," I chimed in. "My blind date days are long gone," I added. "I'll deliver Eve and I'm betting Stu will book his girl, Lynn."

"Our concern is that Amber and Sonya from last year will probably make your little make-believe dates look even worse than them."

"They're not even in Lynn's league," Stuart told them. "And even if Simon is pushing up on that easy-bake-oven cook from D & B's, she'd be better than them."

"*My* Eve doesn't have anything to do with some stupid easy-bake oven." I remarked. "In fact, she's so fine, I bet she can't even cook."

"And what's that supposed to mean?" Rod said forcefully. "Are you saying that my Grace can't cook?"

"He never said your Grace was fine," Stuart blurted out, starting to laugh.

On any other day, I would have jumped right in with Stuart. He'd scored big-time on Rod. And what made it worse was that he was right. Grace wasn't too hard on the eyes. In fact, I'd even say she was cute. But "fine" wasn't exactly how you'd describe her in a police report. Stu had an uncanny way of attacking the best of them and then cruising to another topic before the victim had a chance to fully understand that he'd been insulted. But this wasn't one of those times. Rod had a bug up his ass about something and Stuart was about to get bit.

"You little MF!" Rod yelled, charging toward Stuart. "I'll kick your ass, your dead grandmomma's ass and her dead grandmomma's ass too."

"You can kick my ass all you want to," Stuart shot back, making certain to hide behind both me and Trevor, "but all the ass whipping in the world ain't about to make your wife fine."

"Let go of me!" Rod exclaimed, trying to tear our hands away. "I'll tear his heart out."

"Back off, Rod," I said, holding my hands as if they were a cross.

"What the hell is this?" Trevor asked, shocked. "Do you think he's a vampire or a werewolf or something?"

"I don't know who the hell he thinks he is but y'all better hold him back before I step to him," Stuart told us.

"What?!" Trevor and I yelled, together. "Have you lost your mind?!"

And that's all Rod needed. He broke loose and attacked Stuart like he owned him.

"You think you're slick because you got a degree?!" Rod exclaimed, starting to choke him. "Say something slick now, college boy!"

Stuart was at a loss for words. But I'm certain Rod's mas-

Van Whitfield

sive hands planted firmly around his neck had something to do with that. We had to do something.

"Chill out, Rod!" I yelled, reaching for his hands. "You know Grace is fine," I said, tugging. "He's just jealous because he can't find someone like her."

"Yeah, buddy," Trevor told him, also grabbing his hands. "You can't let a jerk like him get you upset like this."

"Damn, Rod," Stuart said, gasping for air as we pulled him away. "You know I was just BS-ing," he told him. "Grace is fine two times," he lied.

I didn't know what the hell was going on. I'd never seen Rod this bent out of shape. If he was ever stressed-out, it never showed. As far as we knew, he had the life. A wife he loved. Two beautiful, if not a little too "active," teenaged daughters and a business that earned him a healthy profit year in and year out. What could be the problem? And how could we bring it up without violating his privacy and alienating our buddy?

"What's the deal, Rod?" I asked, looking him in the eye. "Is it Grace?"

"I can't talk about it," he said, standing erect. "No," he added, shaking his head. "I *won't* talk about it."

"You don't have to," Trevor assured him. "But if there's something you need to get out, you know we'll listen."

"What have you guys ever gotten out?" Rod asked, looking us over. "You've never brought anything personal to the table."

He'd hit a spot and he knew it. Our immediate silence and strained stares all but confirmed it. We were buddies and we'd be there for each other through anything. We all knew that. But I was certain that formula worked because besides some petty financial problems before we started investing, we'd never had to be there for each other.

It was a guy thing.

We didn't do the emotional support thing well. Most of us didn't even know it existed. Every guy I knew went through problems. We were all confronted with instances and events that confounded and defeated us. Like women, we got down, depressed and dragged ourselves through bouts of low self-esteem, anxiety and just plain being unhappy. We never knew why women did what they did, why they cheated, connived and lied, just like us, but it impacted on our psyches just like it did on women.

But women knew how to deal with it.

They'd join Friday evening encounter groups and Sunday afternoon book clubs and create all manner of social outlets which gave them a forum to deal with their problems. Women would seek counseling or pray the skin off their knees if it would lead them to peace of mind. And when they'd tried everything they knew of or could imagine, they'd light some candles, lounge around a table and talk. They'd say, "The same thing happened to me," or, "If your momma couldn't trust your daddy, what makes you think you can trust your man?" And it all made sense because even if they slaughtered, belittled and bemoaned men across the board, they were at least addressing their problems, which was something we men didn't do or wouldn't do.

Rod was on point. None of us had ever "gotten it out" with the group. I'd been crushed by women so bad there were mornings I couldn't force myself out of bed. I couldn't accept that someone could find me so disposable. My self-esteem was shattered and living life seemed like an option instead of a gift from God. But what could I do? I couldn't call a buddy to commiserate with me because for my entire life on this planet, I'd never had a buddy call me seeking a heart-to-heart about some woman who'd just blown him away. We didn't do encounter groups on Friday nights because we'd rather be out with a woman we couldn't stand than be marooned to the couch on a Friday night. Sunday afternoon book clubs didn't get it because football and basketball dominated our Sundays and we tended not to read anything that didn't pull out into a centerfold.

And I didn't know one guy who had voluntarily sought out counseling. To us, counseling was a last-ditch effort that was only to be utilized when you wanted to appear like you were interested in saving a relationship, a marriage or a job. It was as if seeking real help was some kind of sworn enemy. We were convinced that if counseling was called for at any level, the situation that needed addressing was probably too far gone. The relationship was kaput. The marriage was done. And the vacancy you were about to create at work was already being filled.

Who needed counseling to figure that out?

I didn't know. But I knew Rod needed something. He looked drained. His eyes were weary and his mammoth hands were trembling. I knew he needed something, but I had no clue as to how to reach him. He didn't want a hug or even one of those patented male bonding–style pats on the back. For the first time in my life I could see that my buddy was in need. But I felt like a helpless chump. And

I'm sure Trevor and Stuart felt the same way, because we all knew there was nothing we could do for him. We knew Rod would never reach out to us, especially since we'd never reached out to him. I was certain neither of us wanted to be the first to acknowledge we had feelings that were more substantial than the self-affirming "I'm cool" or the infamous "I'm not pressed. You know I can handle my business." None of us wanted to carry that burden and risk opening ourselves up to the possibility of ridicule or shame with our buddies. Our pecking order didn't allow for that and Rod was getting screwed because of it. We were failing him. And in the grand order of friendship and being there for those you care about, we failed ourselves.

There was no way we could go on with any type of meeting. I looked over at Stuart and hoped he'd rescue us with some pithy line that would piss off Trevor and ease the tension which now enveloped the room. But when he just shook his head "no," I prepared for the worst. Someone had to lighten the load. And since it was all but pushing my head farther down between my shoulders, I knew it had to be me.

"So, Trevor," I started, still looking at Rod. "This was a blind date thing, huh?"

"Yeah, Simon," he replied, slowly nodding his head. "Even though Stuart is the ultimate ladies' man, we're not interested in another trip like last year. We were going to have Leigh and Grace set you guys up with some really good prospects."

"Really good prospects?!" Stuart exclaimed, bringing us back to some sense of reality. "The last prospects your wife came up with were on parole."

"Well, this will be different," Trevor told us. "We've put the word out and they're setting up a little dinner party for next weekend."

"Who's cooking?" I asked, concerned.

"Is that all you're worried about?" Stuart asked, incensed. "What's on the menu and who's cooking it?"

"The way I see it, we're going to have to sit around with some desperate-ass women who we would never want in the first place, so we might as well eat good and at least get something out of the evening," I answered, watching Rod pace around the room.

"The food will be hot and the women will be hotter," Trevor convinced us, forcing a smile.

"When you tried to set me up with Carla you said she was hot too," Stuart reminded him. "She wore a uniform to work," he added. "And who in their right mind would date a blue collar woman?" he asked. "Plus she had a son, and you know I don't date women with children and babies' daddies."

"Carla was hot," Trevor quickly replied. "And who cares about what she wears to work?" he asked. "Her son's a darling. She was a decent lady. And as I recall, she sang in the church choir."

"And as *I* recall, she was doing Reverend Peters," I said, starting to laugh.

"Yeah, and she was doing Reverend Peters' wife too!" Stuart remarked.

"And what about Lacy?" I asked, shaking my head. "You remember her, Trevor?"

"I most certainly do. Very nice woman. Shapely. Bright. Beautiful eyes—"

"And a husband to die for," Stuart interrupted.

"They were separated," Trevor insisted.

"It's not called separated when you live upstairs and your husband squats in the basement," I commented.

"And it's definitely not separated when you're pregnant by the guy in the basement who just happens to be your husband," Stuart told him.

"She wasn't pregnant," Trevor said, eyeing Rod, who was now seated with his back toward us.

"What are you talking about, Trevor?" Stuart asked, annoyed. "She called me and said she was thinking about naming the baby after me because I was more of a man than the baby's daddy."

"Don't flatter yourself, Stuart. Her husband's one of my patients and he's a good man."

"If he's such a good man, why in the hell did you set Stuart up with his wife?" I asked, staring at Rod.

That question would go unanswered. Rod made sure of that. He sat alone in the corner of the room with his head resting in his hands. We didn't know what to make of it. If he was crying, what were we supposed to do? Hand him a handkerchief? We didn't know. Should we ask him what's wrong again, so he could remind us to mind our business? Or should we respect his privacy and give him space to deal with whatever had him spooked? It was clear we were at as much of a loss as Rod, because we all headed in his direction without a clue as to how to reach him.

"What's shaking, buddy?" Trevor asked, instinctively patting him on the back. "You and Grace have a run-in or something?"

"This just isn't fair," Rod confessed. "We've always been together and been there for each other," he shared. "When she's down I'm up and when I'm down she's up."

"I never knew you got down," Stuart quipped. "I didn't think marines were allowed to roll like that."

"Shut up, Stuart," Trevor begged.

"No one could have ever convinced me that me and Gracie wouldn't last forever, but I saw it with my own eyes," he told us. "It was right there in my face."

"Are you saying what I think you're saying?" I asked, concerned.

"He said he saw it with his own eyes so he has to be saying what you think he's saying," Stuart surmised.

"I can't believe he's saying what I think he's saying," Trevor added, shaking his head in disbelief. "Not Grace."

We were shocked. Make that beyond shocked. Grace was as solid as they come. She was smart enough, cute enough and she was the perfect complement to Rod. Together, they ran their travel agency and raised their daughters with an almost unreal sense of purpose and dignity. We'd never seen them argue or even disagree without resolving it with a quick kiss and a generous hug. We all wanted what Rod had. A wife who was a real friend and a real partner. Leigh and Trevor had more of an understanding than a relationship. Leigh understood her job was to be the beautiful doctor's wife and Trevor understood his role as well. He had to work his ass off so his beautiful wife could keep herself beautiful. But Rod and Grace—they had it all. I think we all felt Grace was different from most of the women we knew. She loved Rod more than he loved himself. So hearing firsthand that she was a cheat and knowing Rod was forced to see it was a first-rate stunner.

"You actually saw it?" Stuart asked, worried.

"I saw it with my own eyes," Rod told us.

"Damn," I said, frustrated. "I can't believe Grace would carry it like that."

"It makes me wonder about Leigh," Trevor confided. "I don't know what I'd do. It almost makes me happy that my attorney convinced her to sign that pre-nup."

"You got Leigh to sign a pre-nup?" Stuart asked, surprised. "You're smarter than I thought."

"He sure is," I remarked. "I always thought Leigh would be the tramp. Not Grace."

"She probably is a tramp," Stuart added. "They're probably somewhere right now, getting their tramps on."

"I never thought we'd see eye to eye on Leigh," Trevor said, nervously pulling out his cell phone. "But you're right. Leigh's probably out with some other guy right now."

Trevor had one of those Nextel phones with a speaker and a feature that allowed you to click in on other users instead of placing a call.

"Leigh!" Trevor yelled. "Pick up the phone now, Leigh!" he insisted.

"Honey, is that you?" she answered.

"Don't 'honey' me," he told her. "Where are you?"

"Is something wrong, sweetheart?" she asked, laying it on thick.

"Do you have me on speaker?" Trevor asked, his right foot nervously tapping.

"Of course I have you on speaker, honey," she answered. "Is everything okay? You sound like you're in a tiff."

"I'm not tiffing," he said awkwardly. "I just want to make sure I'm on speaker because I want whoever is there with *my wife* to know that you have an insanely jealous husband who knows seven different ways to kill a man."

"Name three of them," Stuart said, laughing.

"Who was that?" Leigh asked, concerned. "Is someone there with you?"

"Who's there with *you*?" Trevor asked, topping her. "I bet you're out ..." he added, looking toward Stuart. "What did you say she was doing?" he whispered.

"She's getting her tramp on."

"I bet you're out with some no good sleazeball and you're on a trampoline right now."

"Oh brother," I whispered.

"He's hopeless," Stuart agreed.

Obviously, someone else agreed too. We heard a mountain of laughter come through Trevor's tiny speakerphone. For the quickest of moments I worried that Leigh was stuck at an orgy or an overcrowded love-in because so many people were laughing. But like any good player, she wasted little time straightening things out.

"What's going on, Trevor?" Leigh asked, sounding panicked. "What is this all about."

"It's about you and Grace and cheating and man-izing and our pre-nup," he fired off.

"Man-izing," Stuart whispered. "Is that even a word?"

"He's on a roll," I suggested. "And if 'womanizing' is a word, why wouldn't 'man-izing' be one?"

"Honey, I'm sure everyone here at the salon is amused that you've made a complete fool of yourself," Leigh replied, embarrassed. "Little Trevor's here with me. He's getting a shampoo and I'm getting my thighs waxed," she added. "I don't know what this has to do with our pre-nup, which for the record my attorney says I signed under duress, and I haven't talked to Grace since last night, so I don't know how she plays into this either," she went on. "But if you stop by and pick us up, we'll go grab some sushi and we can clear this whole thing up—okay?" she finished.

"See you in about an hour," Trevor sheepishly responded before clicking off.

We just looked at him like he was the nut we knew him to be.

"So," he said, slipping his phone back into his pants pocket. "At least we know that one of us still has a decent wife," he added, trying to regain composure. "That means there's still hope," he said, noticing Rod was starting to stand.

"I don't know what you're getting at, Trevor," Rod said. "But Grace is great. At least she doesn't have my son prancing around some salon with a bunch of weave-happy yahoos."

"You don't have a son," Trevor reminded him.

"That makes two of you," Stuart joked.

"Look, fellas," Rod said, sounding concerned. "I think you've got the wrong idea."

"How could we?" I asked. "You said you thought you'd be with her forever."

"Yeah," Stuart chimed in. "So that means she screwed up and now you're worried that your pride won't let you stick around."

"You don't have to pretend with us," Trevor assured him. "We already know you saw it with your own eyes. And I know how that must feel. I can't imagine how I'd react if I saw Leigh with another man."

"You'd kill him," Stuart casually recited.

"You'd kill seven different ways, to be exact," I added.

"What other man?" Rod blared out.

"The other man you saw her with," Stuart replied.

"I didn't see Grace with another man," Rod insisted.

"Are you saying you saw her with another woman?" Stuart asked, looking him in the eye.

"There wasn't anybody else!" Rod answered. "This is about me."

"Wait a minute," Trevor jumped in. "You're telling us Grace hired a PI to trail you and that he showed you pictures of you with some other woman."

"I didn't even know he was cheating," I commented, surprised.

"Dig it," Stuart added, smiling. "But I bet she was like that."

"Nobody was like anything," Rod asserted. "I didn't see what you think I saw."

"So what did you see?" Trevor asked, taking a seat.

"I saw the test results at my doctor's office," Rod explained. "I don't know what to do. I don't know how to explain this to Grace," he confessed.

"What is it, Rod?" Stuart asked, worried.

"Just tell us," I begged. "We'll do anything we can."

"What the hell can you do?" he asked, unimpressed. "Look at me," he demanded, grabbing my arm. "I'm gonna die, Simon," he said. Tears began to stream down his face. "I have cancer."

chapter 14

He's Fallen and
He Can't Get It Up

Moments Later

Simon

hat are you talking about, Rod?"

"What type of cancer is it?"

"There goes the trip."

That's all we could muster up. One of our best friends announced he had cancer and we had no clue as to how to respond. I heard what he told us, but it was unacceptable coming from Rod. If you threw us on an island and had the audience vote one person off each week, Rod would be the survivor week in and week out. That's how strong a person and personality he was. I literally couldn't absorb what he'd just told us.

The MD came out in Trevor. He had to know what type of cancer Rod was dealing with. I knew he meant well, but Trevor sincerely believed he was the brightest doctor roaming the planet and that he could solve problems that others couldn't.

And Stuart's response was classic Stuart. If Rod having cancer meant he didn't have to deal with Mexico's drinking water or producing a date for the trip, he might very well rationalize that cancer had an appreciable upside.

"I have prostate cancer," Rod confessed.

"How did you catch that?" Stuart asked, shaking his head.

"You don't catch it, it develops," Trevor told him.

"Did your doctor catch it early?" I asked, stunned. "Marion Barry caught his early and I hear he's fully recovered."

"I don't believe that 'fully recovered' and 'Marion Barry' are terms which belong in the same sentence," Trevor replied.

"You're a doctor, T," Stuart said, walking toward Trevor. "Does this mean the big fella won't be able to get it up anymore?"

Stuart, as usual, struck again.

But this time he didn't mean it. He asked the single most relevant question that crossed any man's mind when he heard the term "prostate cancer." It's as if it were a sentence to death. Guys didn't want to suffer with *anything* that could potentially affect or complicate their potency, virility or sex life. If a guy was on life support after a horrific accident and was told he was paralyzed below the waist, his first thought would be, *Can I still get it up?* And if his doctor was a "him" and gave the patient that much-feared sympathetic head shake "no," the wounded man would waste little time invoking the fateful request, "If I won't be able to get it up, just pull the plug, doc."

This didn't mean the guy was a sex fiend or some kind of pervert. That's not what it was about. It spoke to the fact that a man's sexuality was primarily defined by both the size and operating capacity of his male organ. And if he came up short in either area, he was generally considered as less than a man. Ask a woman about her worst sexual experience and it usually involved some pathetic guy who couldn't get it up or who failed to possess anything worth getting up. She'd giggle and recall when she told her friends how she summarily ran "peewee" out of her bed and out of her life. And she might even go as far as demonstrating "peewee's" approximate size (or lack thereof) by holding her fingers half an inch apart. Women religiously claimed size didn't matter and that what happened in the bedroom was relative when stacked against the entirety of a relationship, but men knew that was crap. Give a woman a mediocre relationship with lights-on, ho-hum sex and you'd be dismissed without fanfare. But women had an uncanny knack of surviving and even justifying relationships that totally sucked if they had lights out, candle-burning, bump and grind romps between the sheets.

It was a simple equation and it didn't make her a sex fiend or some sort of pervert. It just meant that like many men, she was seeking satisfaction. And if a man couldn't satisfy a woman or if he was simply not *packing*, "peewee" (as usual) knew he'd be sent *packing*.

"Are you kidding?" Trevor said, trying to lighten the mood. "Rod here is a stud. He'll be just fine."

"We knew that," I answered, patting him on the back. "Not even the big C can slow this here man down."

"My bad, Rod," Stuart acknowledged, nodding his head. "I just wanted to make sure a brother could still get his swerve on."

"Don't sweat it, Stu," Rod said, half-heartedly slapping him five. "For once your sorry ass is right," he added, now slowly shaking his head. "I haven't been able to 'handle my business' for three months now," he shared. "I'll probably never get it up again."

"Are you saying that you and Grace haven't—" I started to ask.

"You haven't spanked your—" Trevor interrupted, surprised.

"I know the trip is off now," Stuart repeated, sounding relieved.

I couldn't believe it. What were we supposed to say? I hadn't "handled my business" for two months myself. In fact, I was in the midst of a drought that would make a three-hump Moroccan camel cringe. But I didn't have a wife I adored and a slamming DVD porn collection at my disposal either. When one of your buddies confessed to essentially losing his manhood, it was sometimes a cause to gloat or even celebrate. You knew he was as lost as you and that you weren't the last man on the planet who couldn't get laid. But when your buddy announced he had prostate cancer *and* that his sex life had taken a plunge, high-fives and Bud weren't in order. You literally felt his pain, and found yourself checking to make certain *your* tools were still in order.

And noticing that both Trevor and Stuart were checking their goods like I was probably pained Rod even further.

"I want to see you in my office first thing in the morning," Trevor insisted.

"I don't think so," Rod answered.

"I don't blame you," Stuart told him. "You guys are truly my boys," he added. "But I don't think I'd want either one of you inspecting my products."

"I don't think none of us want to inspect your products," I replied, holding back a laugh. "But then again, I don't own a magnifying glass, so that probably counts me out."

We all laughed, which is exactly what we needed. Rod had hit us where it hurts. He had cancer, but I sensed that collectively, we were hurting just as much as he was. No one would want a fate as cruel as cancer for a friend. It was even tougher when you didn't know what to do for that friend. But when all else failed, nothing beat a good laugh.

"Look, fellas," Rod said, still chuckling. "I made a big mistake with this—my doctor says that I let it go too far. There's nothing I can do," he confessed, turning serious. "I started having symptoms almost a year ago. But I didn't think much of it."

"So how did it hit you?"

"The first time I really knew something was wrong was when I couldn't stop going to the bathroom."

"That's a sure sign," Trevor acknowledged.

"Then I just ignored it and figured the symptoms would just go away," he admitted. "But it just got worse."

"And how long did that go on?"

"Five, maybe six months," he guessed. "You know how it is. Guys don't do the doctor thing until it's too late."

"Tell me about it," I agreed. "Mechanics, doctors and lawyers are one in the same."

"If you see them for maintenance, they'll find something wrong, so you might as well wait until you've totally blown it so that they can't screw you over," Stuart chimed in.

"Look, I'm not going to just let you dog out my profession," Trevor interrupted. "It's a patient's responsibility to get to us before the problem gets too far gone."

"He's right," Rod confirmed. "If I had jumped on this from day one, I might not be in this position right now, but I thought I was superman. Nothing was going to put me down."

"So what made you realize you needed help, Rod?"

"I came home one night and Grace had on a teddy that would have made Victoria give up all of her secrets," he said, half-smiling. "And blam!" he exclaimed, his voice trailing off. "I couldn't get things going."

"How did you handle it?" I asked, concerned.

"Are you kidding?" he scoffed. "I blamed it on her."

"And how did she handle it?"

"She was okay the first time," he went on. "But after the third time, she was convinced I was having an affair."

"That's a joke," Stuart laughed.

"That's what I told her, but she wasn't having it," he said. "She started smelling my shirts for perfume and checking my pockets, she even went through my cell phone bill."

"So how did she react when you finally told her what was going on?"

"I haven't told her yet," he admitted. "And I'm not sure that I will," he added.

"That's not the way to go, Rod," Trevor told him. "She's your wife. She deserves to know."

"What she deserves is every ounce of love I can muster," Rod asserted. "I'm not about to take the melodramatic route, but I honestly don't have that much time," he continued. "And I don't want her or you guys throwing me any pity-parties," he added. "Just promise me one thing," he requested.

Then he slowly put his hand out and looked each of us in the eye.

"Be my friend."

"Always," I told him, placing my hand on top of his.

"Always," Stuart repeated, joining in.

"Always," Trevor said, his hand now atop the pile. "And in all ways," he whispered.

We stood in a circle with our hands on top of Rod's in complete silence. With our heads lowered we prayed. And I'm certain each of us replayed the many warm and wonderful moments we'd shared with Rod. I begged God to watch over him and to do all he could for my buddy. I heard Stuart say over and over, "Not Rod, man . . . anybody but Rod." Trevor solemnly recited the Lord's prayer and asked God to keep Rod, Grace and the twins together forever.

Our prayers and requests may have been separate but our fear and agony were one in the same. Why would God take the best of us from us? How would we manage without the glue of our group to keep us together? And how would Grace and the girls survive without knowing that Rod's huge shoulders, which could seemingly carry the weight of the world—how would they go on, knowing they'd never again be able to lean on those shoulders again?

Our minds raced with a million questions.

And the tears covering our faces said to me that the answers might forever elude us.

Grace was about to lose her loyal husband and Kokeisha and Lokeisha were about to lose their beloved dad.

I didn't like keeping Grace out of the loop, but I understood. Rod wanted to be remembered as a strong, tough and determined man. He didn't want a soul on this earth to feel sorry for him or sorry with him. He wanted to die in the same way he lived, with purpose and with dignity.

And in the midst of what had to be one of the toughest moments of his life, he had but one simple request.

That we remain his friends.

We wanted to stay strong for Rod, much as he had been strong for us throughout the years. We owed him. And if God's plan said that Rod's days were indeed numbered, he'd spend each and every one of them with the knowledge that our friendship was deep-rooted and unconditional.

We'd be his friends and he'd be ours.

Always.

chapter 15

Promises, Promises

The Next Day

Stuart

Want to know how it felt to be in Hiroshima back in 1945? Spend an evening with a friend who announces he's about to die. Take away the mushroom cloud and that's what you have—either way, all you're left with is devastation. I'd barely slept wondering about Rod and his dilemma. I wouldn't have wanted to be in his shorts for any reason in the world, but as crazy as it sounds, I would have traded places with him in a minute if it meant he'd be okay.

The one good thing that came out of our meeting was

our reconnecting as a group. Over the years things happened and it was easy to lose sight of what was really important. Friends got married, jobs grew into careers and losing touch was far easier than forcing the issue and maintaining relationships. Because our investment group had flourished, we pretty much only met to discuss our money and how to make more of it. Our big vacation evolved out of a need to stay connected as friends and not just business partners. Trevor and Leigh had their screwed-up life with little Trevor, and Rod and Grace had their hands full with each other and the twins. But all Simon and I had was each other. And Rod's admission had driven the point home harder than we could handle. I guess that's why I invited Simon over for breakfast.

"What's up, Stu?" he asked, walking into my living room.

"Not me," I admitted. "I hardly slept last night."

"Who could?" he asked, taking up nearly two spots on the couch.

"I just wonder how Rod slept," I told him.

"Rod probably slept like a king," he answered, smiling. "After he kicked us out, he probably worked out, hit the Jacuzzi and crashed before Grace got home."

"I wonder."

"You wonder what?" he asked. "If he was asleep before Grace rolled in?"

"No," I started. "I wonder how he deals with it," I said, walking toward the kitchen. "I wonder if it hurts and what it really feels like to summon the troops and they can't answer."

"You know Rod," he replied, his head nodding. "He's so

strong-willed he's probably not feeling anything," he added. "And as for summoning the troops," he said, before pausing. "If we don't keep our word, Rod'll probably see to it that we won't have any troops to summon."

As we laughed and headed for the kitchen, I considered that Simon was right. Before we left, Rod swore us to one final request. He demanded that we make this year's trip the biggest and the best yet. "This'll be my last one," he told us. "And while I'm waiting for you fools to cash in your tickets to heaven, I want to have at least one good memory to hold me over."

And after that he made a request that stunned us all.

"Simon," he started. "I have one wish. I want you to promise me that your girl Kit Kat is going to be on the trip."

"If that's all you want, you know I won't let you down. She'll be there no matter what," Simon assured him. "But remember—Kit Kat is history. Her name is Eve."

"Eve," Rod answered, then turned toward me. "And you, Stu," he went on. "I know you wouldn't deny a dying man his last wish," he said convincingly. "I want your word that this Lynn who we've never seen will be on the trip too."

"I'm two steps ahead of you," I told him. "I guarantee it," I continued. "Nothing will keep me from having Lynn on that trip."

Nothing except me.

And that was precisely my problem. My landing Lynn for the trip was an iffy proposition at best. And my gut told me Simon was probably as bad off with Eve. Rod had raised the stakes for both of us. Breaking a promise to a true friend was tough. But denying a friend his last wish was like landing in no-man's-land, because no man would want to be there. We were going to deliver the goods. We owed Rod as much. And we had about two weeks to make it happen, so no one was going to keep me and Lynn away from Cancun. Including me.

"So, Simon," I said, joining him at my dining room table. "When I was out with Lynn the other night, you know I almost had her booked for the trip."

"Explain to me exactly how someone *almost* gets somebody else booked for a trip," he said sarcastically.

"Okay," I answered. "So maybe she wasn't almost booked. But I would have booked her if she had given me the chance."

"I feel the same way about Eve," Simon told me. "But she has this whole control thing going so getting a read on her isn't the easiest thing in the world."

"I know just what you mean. It's not like I want a relationship with Lynn, but if I take two steps toward her, she's taking three steps back," I replied, cracking open a boiled egg. "It's like she wants to know me, but she doesn't want me to know her."

"That's Eve," Simon agreed. "We could spend an entire evening together and I'd know more about her at the start than I would at the end."

"I asked Lynn where she was from once and you know what she told me?"

"It doesn't matter," he answered, chewing on a slice of bacon.

"Right."

"And if you ask her about her family—" he started.

"Doesn't exist," I replied, reaching for some salt.

"I think it's a nineties thing that carried over into the new millennium," he reasoned. "Women want the upper hand and if they get it they're not giving it up."

Simon couldn't have been more on point. The nineties saw women leap ahead when it came to careers and secondary education. Women appeared to be as career driven and as focused as men when it came to performance and the rewards reaped from a job well done. Corporate boardrooms were no longer single-sex facilities run by men for men. There were more women roaming college campuses than men. Old-school Neanderthals still thought they were in charge, but their stockholders and marketing firms were well aware that women were really running things.

Especially relationships.

It's as if women scientifically gathered data and concluded that the only way to beat men was to join them. So instead of sitting around waiting for the phone to ring, women were online, mapping out their dates and their weekends. And when you took her out, she was reaching in her wallet to pay the bill because she wanted it to be crystal clear that she owed you absolutely nothing. If anything, you owed her and she wanted you to know it.

Why do you think so many chick-flicks had hit the local cineplex, while shoot-'em-up thrillers had hit the skids? Because women now decided what we'd see and why we'd see it. Did you really believe your lady dragged you to see *How Stella Got Her Groove Back* because she thought you needed to see Taye Diggs shake his million dollar ass in the shower? Heck no. It was a warning. The shape of things to come.

Before you knew it she'd spill the beans about that little trip to the islands she and her friends had been planning for years. And because you were a cocky, overconfident guy you'd fall for it. You'd even help her pick out a nice one-piece bathing suit, but her friends were the ones who'd help her with a seductive bikini. And before you drove her to the airport you'd have a flashback to *Stella* and you'd foolishly ask, "You're not going down there to get *your* groove back are you?"

"Of course not, silly," she'd answer, handing you back your wallet. "That only happens in the movies."

And she'd conveniently leave out the fact that Terry McMillan was living proof that the mating game was alive and well down in the islands because she actually married the movie.

"You know something, Simon," I said, picking up a glass of orange juice. "I'm taking the upper hand. Lynn is going on this trip."

"So what's your plan?" Simon asked, buttering some toast.

"That's why you're here," I answered. "I figure between the two of us, something has to shake right."

"I got you," he replied. "So here's the deal," he started. "Call Lynn and tell her you have to see her tonight."

"And why would I *have* to see her?" I asked, unimpressed. "It's not like I can force her over here by having her think I'm pregnant or something."

"Right," he answered. "Women use that racket all the time," he told me. "It goes right back to that control thing. They even have better excuses than we do," he stated. "But face it, Stu, you've got to create some urgency."

"I'll play the vulnerable role," I reasoned. "I'll tell her I just need somebody to talk to."

"What are you, a woman?"

"I'm just trying to figure out some excuse to get her here," I admitted. "I don't want her to start thinking that I'm trying to reel her in."

"What is she, a fish?" he exclaimed. "Forget the excuse," he said, smiling, "How's her appetite?"

"She's not one of those fake 'I'm just having a salad,' babes," I shared. "But it's not like she eats like you either."

"Good," he answered. "So hit her with the old 'I want to make you dinner' move."

"You might have something there, Simon," I answered, heading to the fridge. "I could lure her in with my lobster ravioli or some all-lump-crab cakes."

"But first you have to slip on some of that smooth Pat Metheny and pop open some vino-vino," he advised.

"And I've got to do the candle thing," I realized. "She has to know I have something special in mind."

"Break out one of those slamming shrimp and chicken Caesar salads you made last Thanksgiving. But go heavy on the dressing."

"And I'll do up some of those garlic-butter biscuits."

"Don't forget your vicious cream of crab soup."

"Nothing fancy for dessert though," I added, slapping him high five. "Just the best damn sweet-potato cheese-cake this side of the Mississippi."

"And Cancun here we come!" we yelled, together.

"So what's your plan, Simon?" I asked, arranging bowls on my kitchen cooking island. "How are you going to con Eve into going?"

"I'm not trying to con her," he answered. "I don't see Eve as just a date for a trip," he confessed. "I want the real thing from her. Time. A commitment. A house on the hill. I'm like Warren G.," he told me, smiling. "I want it all."

"So how you gonna get it?" I asked.

"I'm doing exactly what you're doing."

"You're not a cook, Simon," I reminded him.

"Who needs to be a cook when I've got you around?"

"I got you, big fella," I said, smiling.

"You're already cooking, so just double up on everything and it's on."

"Aren't you eating?" I asked, reaching for the phone.

"Of course," he answered.

"Then I'd better *triple-up* on everything," I joked.

"That's a good idea," he said, rubbing his stomach. "Especially that sweet-potato cheesecake."

"Hello," Lynn answered, picking up the phone.

"Lynn, I need someone to talk to," I sheepishly uttered.

"What are you, a woman?" she asked, starting to laugh.

"What I meant to say is that you need somebody to talk to," I said, sounding even stupider than I just sounded.

"What you need is to sit yourself down, think about what you're saying and call me back when you get yourself together," she calmly stated.

"I'm straight," I said, trying to play it cool. "I have an idea," I told her.

"So shoot," she told me. "Let's hear it."

"Crabcakes, champagne and candlelight."

"How clever. Now can you do that with three words starting with another letter?"

"Salad and sex at seven."

"That's an interesting combination, but I think I get your point," she said. "And just where shall I meet you at seven?"

"My place," I answered, shooting Simon a thumbs-up. "I'll play chef and all you'll need is your appetite."

"I like that. Seven it is," she whispered.

I couldn't believe it was that easy. Simon was right. As soon as I got to the point, she was all for it. I couldn't have drawn it up any better. Now I knew I could get her on the trip. But I worried about Simon. He wasn't nearly as smooth as me. He'd fall all over himself and start losing focus. I had to get him pumped. He needed to call just like me and he had to do it now while I was around to push him.

"Okay, Mr. Big Stuff," I said, handing him the phone. "Call Eve and work your magic."

"I'll call her later," he said, pausing. "It's kind of early, right?"

"It wasn't too early for me to call Lynn."

"But what if she's not home?" he asked, concerned.

"Leave a message. That's even better."

"What the hell," he muttered, hitting the talk button. "All she can do is turn me down."

"Do me a favor," I said, peeling some sweet potatoes for the cheesecake. "Hit star 67 and block my number. If Eve has some whacked-out boyfriend or something, I don't want him getting my number and calling me back."

"If she's dealing with somebody else, I'll put my size-twelves straight up his tailbone."

"Ouch!" I said, laughing.

"Evey-eve," Simon said, smoothly. "Check this. What time can you get over to my place tonight?"

He winked at me and gave me a thumbs-up. I just hope she doesn't turn him down.

"That's a plan. Hit me when you finish up with your meeting and we'll make it happen," he told her. "Late," he said, before hanging up.

"She's with it?" I asked, surprised.

"She has a meeting, but she's rolling through after that," he told me. "So that will give me some extra time to pull things together."

"You're right, Simon," I said, breaking open some eggs. "Could you hand me that paprika?"

"You know something, Stu," Simon said, starting to leave. "We may not have much time to pull this off, but something tells me it's going to happen. Trevor's going to be shocked and Rod's going to be proud," he remarked, slapping me five. "Cancun is looking pretty good right about now," he added, smiling. "Especially since we're gonna keep those promises."

"I can't wait to see Lynn in a thong," I told him.

"You'll forget all about Ms. Lynn when you see Eve in a thong," Simon bragged. "I'm going to see if I can get my maid service to get to my place this afternoon."

"When did you get a maid service?" I asked, watching him stroll to his Rover.

"When I figured it was a good way to get a woman to stop through," he laughed.

That's not a bad idea, I thought, closing the door. *She cleans, she doesn't bore you about her rotten day and she leaves before you know it,* I considered. *Why isn't every woman a maid?*

chapter 16

Stuart Hits the Jackpot

Later That Evening

Stuart

Pleated silk trousers. A cream-colored five-button silk shirt. And my favorite tan suede Gucci slip-ons. The perfect complement to the perfect meal. Simon hit the jackpot with this one. I would have never thought of inviting Lynn over for dinner. Women like her usually demanded to be courted in "the manner to which they'd become accustomed." Which basically meant that wining and dining started with expensive champagne and ended with desserts that looked much better than they tasted.

Each and every time Lynn had been to my place

we started and ended in one place—the bedroom. She often left while I was still knocked out as a result of our incredible lovemaking. And other times, she insisted that I drop her back at her job because she wanted to check on the overnight, overseas markets. I'd never been to her place, but that was okay. I'd spent the better part of my adult life trying mightily to keep women away from my spot, so I actually respected and appreciated her desire for privacy.

But tonight she was going to get a new lesson in *my* brand of privacy. After I made certain that every aspect of the meal was in perfect order, I sat down at my dining room table and devised a written and wonderfully detailed nineteen-point date strategy that read:

1. Turn off the telephone. (The wrong interruption could blow the whole evening.)
2. Turn on the musical mood setter: Pat Metheny's *Still Life (Talking)* CD.
3. Mention trip.
4. Offer champagne and toast to a wonderful evening. (She'll get tipsy, and you *know* what's next!)
5. Comment on her wardrobe. Practice and select one from below.
    A. "That dress is remarkable."
    B. "That outfit is exquisite."
    C. "That color's nice, but it's not as beautiful as your eyes."
    D. "You look almost as good as me."
6. Offer hors d'oeuvres: crab balls. (Buff the silver platter from Tiffany's.)

7. Mention trip.

8. Light candles. (Let her help—establishes sense of togetherness.)

9. Move to dining room. (Slide out her chair, spread napkin across her lap.)

10. Mention trip.

11. Present food on domed silver platter.

12. Insist on dessert. (Tell her it won't mess with her beautiful figure—try to sound genuine.)

13. Mention trip.

14. Bring out coffee.

15. Get commitment on trip.

16. Sex (optional).

    A. If good, reaffirm her commitment to trip.

    B. If mediocre, see 17, below.

17. Sleep (in event of 16 B).

18. Make sure remote is on my side of bed.

19. Ask if she'd ever consider being a maid (ha-ha!).

It might seem over the top, but entertaining a woman at home had come to this. I was a pro at it, but I usually couldn't care less about making a good impression. Lynn was the perfect woman for the trip because she'd go about her business when it was over, so I couldn't leave one single detail to chance.

There was a time, perhaps even as late as the early 1980s, when dating was flat-out fun. Disco was slowly fading, but nightclubs were still places to dance and to have a good time. One-night stands weren't out of the question and penicillin was an available and effective ally. Women hadn't started hiring private detectives to get the scoop on you before you were ready to offer up information on your own. And you could actually have a first date where you didn't have to bring your resume and credit report or recite your long-term objectives in regard to relationships and matrimony.

But now things were totally different. When you showed up at a woman's house, you could count on a near-pitch-perfect date. Thanks to PCs, the Internet and specialized date-planning software, the evening's events would transpire with awe-inspiring precision. It was no mistake that the wine had been chilled to perfection or that the microwave would beep the very moment you tired of the delicately prepared fruit and cheese plate. Your seemingly unassuming date would have every course within hand's reach before you finished the preceding course. And your input to the "follow-up festivities" in the bedroom would be limited in ways you might never understand, because she had already decided whether or not you'd get a piece long before you arrived.

This all happened because when it came to dating, women got it. They prepared with the ferocity of an NBA basketball coach during the play-offs because they understood that the best-laid plans many times garner the very best of results. Women were fully aware that first impressions are lasting. So preparing every aspect of a date took on a heightened urgency, because if you were impressed enough, you'd foolishly want to share her incredible skills for entertaining and hospitality with your family and friends. Instead of realizing you'd been all but had, you'd foolishly think, *She really knows how to set out a spread. My mom would love her during the holidays. And she'd make my buddies feel like kings when we have a fight party.*

It was a wonderful game of give and take. And now men found themselves playing the very same game. The days of inviting a woman over and not having your place straight and the meal planned out were long gone. Guys were now evaluated on every aspect of the evening. So coming correct was of extreme importance because if the evening was a success the man was less of a target. The woman surmised that you didn't need her to manage your household or any social gatherings you might host. She saw you could take care of yourself, so she backed off ever so slightly and allowed the relationship to progress at a natural pace. And the fact that you cared enough to plan the evening said to her that she was special, because she knew you didn't set out gourmet spreads for your booty-call babes who settled for hot dogs—literally.

And that's what I needed Lynn to know—that going on this trip would make her special and would give her a leg up on the many other women vying for my attention. Waiting for seven o'clock had been quite the adventure. I'd already taped my date list to the fridge and had adjusted my clothes in the mirror more often than Cindy Crawford on a fashion shoot. I recited the list over and over. The evening had to go exactly as planned, because I had no real backup and no other options to get her on the trip. I couldn't just come out and say, "Hey, you up for a trip to Cancun?" That would be playing her cheap and women like Lynn simply didn't fall for that. But since the clock on my wall had just hit seven and the doorbell was ringing like the bell for a heavyweight title fight, I headed to the door with my spirits and my plan intact. All I had to do

was stick to my plan and she'd have one foot in Cancun before we got to dessert.

Hi, handsome," she said, as I opened the door. "Don't you
look sharp."

"Yeah," I answered, already forgetting what I was supposed to say. "Would you mind if I ran in the kitchen a
second?"

"Sure," she answered, making her way toward the
couch. "I hope you remembered to turn off the phone. We
don't want any interruptions from your little harem."

How did she know about the harem? I wondered, walking to the refrigerator and reading from the list. *And how
did she know the phone was the first thing on the list?*

"Stuart," she called from the living room. "How about
a little music while you get things together?" she asked.
"Do you still have that Pat Metheny CD I like?"

Still Life (Talking). I said to myself, concerned. *She's two
for two. Who the hell told her about the list?*

"You must have read my mind," I said, trying to play it
smooth. "I'll be right out," I added, grabbing a tray of
lightly broiled crab balls.

Remember, I thought, walking back into the living
room. *Compliment the outfit, compliment the outfit. Pick one
and go with it.*

"So, Lynn," I said, offering her a crab ball. "I know this
is out of order—"

"Out of order?" she asked, surprised.

"What I meant to say is that it's not like I have a list or
anything, so I'm not going in any certain order."

"Don't tell me that God's gift to womankind is tongue-tied," she remarked, dipping a tiny crab ball into my home-made seafood dressing. "Because what I'm hearing is that you have a list and that you've somehow managed to lose track even though I've only been here for a hot minute."

"List?" I asked, alarmed. "I don't have any list," I lied. "Did I mention your wardrobe?" I asked, flustered.

"My wardrobe?" she replied, starting to grin. "I think you mean my clothes," she added. "And if I'm not mistaken, you're supposed to compliment my outfit *before* the hors d'oeuvres."

"That's not what my list says," I stupidly admitted.

"I thought you didn't have a list."

"What I was saying was that if I *had* a list, the compliment would come after the hors d'oeuvres."

"Oh, really. And what would follow the hors d'oeuvres?"

"Would you mind if I ran to the kitchen for a second?"

I was a mess. First of all, I'd already retreated to the kitchen twice and I still hadn't turned off the phone, which was the first thing I was supposed to do. The musical mood setter, which was the second item set for my "perfect date," was nowhere to be found. So I was two steps down. "Mention the trip" was the third task, but was it politically correct to go to the third item when you'd failed so miserably on the first two? And what about the outfit? She was right! I was supposed to hit her with the compliment *before* the stupid hors d'oeuvres. This date was barely five minutes old, and already it was totally screwed. What made it worse was that she knew I'd blown it, which meant she'd think I'd really need her to manage my social gatherings, so instead of a date for the trip, I was about to get stuck with a wife.

When nothing was on the line, I was usually well atop the crowd when it came to women. But when I had something to lose, I could be as lost as the next schlub. This date couldn't get any worse. At least that's what I was thinking—when the phone started ringing.

"I told you," she said from the living room. "You should have turned that phone off."

"I'll get it and I'll be right out," I said, reaching for a bottle of champagne. "Hello," I said, answering the phone.

"Stu, baby. What's up?"

It was Simon.

"She there?" he asked.

"That's an understatement," I answered, locating two long-stemmed glasses. "She's out in the living room."

"So what's the verdict? How's she look?"

"I screwed that part up," I confessed.

"You did what?"

"I was supposed to tell her how she looked before the hors d'oeuvres, but I forgot, so she got the crab balls before I could tell her about her outfit," I told him.

"You made crab balls?" he asked, excited. "You didn't send any with the spread you made for Eve and me."

"How can you think about food at a time like this?" I asked, upset. "I'm flaming here."

"You burned the food?" he asked, upset. "I haven't even checked mine yet," he told me. "Please tell me you didn't burn the sweet-potato cheesecake."

"Simon," I nervously stated. "You are no help!" I exclaimed. "None!"

"Are you going to be much longer?" Lynn asked.

"It's just one of those phone solicitors," I answered,

starting to hang up. "He was doing a poll about my eating habits."

"I don't think that's on the list," she said sarcastically.

"Neither do I!" I exclaimed, slamming down the phone. "Good night, sir."

I needed a comeback. A way to reclaim the evening and win back some respect. Even though it was completely out of order, complimenting her outfit was the way to go. It would allow her to see that although I'd been confronted with an obstacle, I knew how to establish control as well as maintain my wits. And more important, a well-placed compliment would illustrate to her that I not only knew a decent outfit when I saw one, but it would speak to my appreciation for her wardrobe selection for our date. I'd pick one, commit it to memory and deliver it so smoothly, she'd ask *me* to go on a trip.

I walked into the living room, planted myself down beside her, popped open a well-aged bottle of Cristal champagne and considered exactly which compliment would work best.

"Hey, Lynn," I said, handing her a glass.

She wasted little time downing the entire glass and then holding it up for a refill. I immediately recalled Lynn's extreme lack of tolerance when it came to liquor, especially champagne. I never knew what I'd get when she drank, though I remembered her style of drinking very closely resembled that of a trench-coat-wearing, panhandling lush. Unlike most of the women I knew, I'd never seen her lightly sip and converse while drinking socially. When it came to booze, Lynn went whole hog. She essentially sucked her drinks down like they were big gulps attached to a vacuum system. And within a matter of moments she'd announce, "I hope you don't mind, but I think I'm tipsy."

"Yes, Stuart," she answered, her words already starting to slur. "What would you like to tell me?" she added, leaning her head against my shoulder.

"About that outfit."

"Yes," she replied before downing her second glass in one smooth gulp.

"You look almost as good as me."

"You are too funny," she answered, starting to fan herself. "Did you just turn on the heat or something?" she asked. "And whatever happened to the music?" she went on.

"The music," I said, standing and then heading toward my entertainment center. "Pat Metheny to the rescue."

"Do you really think I look almost as good as you?" she asked, sounding downright plastered after just two drinks.

"Even better," I answered, walking back to the couch.

"Good," she happily answered. "That means you'll dance with me."

I would have danced with her no matter what she looked like. She slumped into my arms and we engaged ourselves in an act that, on some truly insane level, could be considered dancing. We turned in slow circles and I knew I had to make a move. I was certain she would be sound asleep in a matter of minutes. My well-planned date was falling short of even my most meager expectations. But I reasoned that this could all be working to my advantage. I still had time to sober her up with the lobster ravioli and by the time I got to dessert, she'd be all but booked for the trip. It was time to hint around and at least see if she was open to the idea.

"So, Lynn," I said, holding her arm up.

"You look almost as good as you," she blurted out.

"I was thinking—do you like to travel?"

"I love to travel."

"Me and a group of friends are putting together this lit-tle trip. Actually we do it every year, but this year is spe-cial," I shared.

"Your friends are going to be there?"

"Of course," I told her. "It's a group thing."

"Well, I've never done that before," she told me, her words now totally joining one another.

"So you're in?" I asked, surprised.

"Of course," she answered, sloppily nodding her head. "Let's go."

"It's not for a few weeks," I remarked.

"What's not for a few weeks?" she asked, tilting her head back.

"The trip."

"I thought you said we were traveling," she remarked. "You said it was a group thing with your friends."

"It is."

"So why are we still standing here?" she asked, standing back and placing her hands on her hips. "We have to get moving so we can do the group thing with your friends."

"What are you talking about, Lynn?"

"The trip to your bedroom," she answered, smiling se-ductively. "I hope you don't mind," she whispered, draw-ing close to my ear. "But I think I'm tipsy."

That's all I needed to hear. Her being *tipsy* was much better than her passing out drunk. I could make things happen in the bedroom, sell her on the trip and still manage to catch "SportsCenter." We hurried to the bedroom and wasted little time undressing. I knew a condom was in order, so I headed for the bathroom and wondered if she was really up for the group thing. And if she really was up for it, I couldn't help but wonder if *I* was. It took me just a few seconds to locate a three-pack, which, miserably, had sat unopened and unused for far too long.

As I headed back into the bedroom, I thought of the many nights I was fortunate enough to catch Lynn when she was tipsy. She was an absolutely incredible lover, which worried me. I hadn't been with a woman in over a month. I read this article on tantric sex and it convinced me that "preservation" was the first step toward achieving a heightened sense of sexual enlightenment. I wasn't pulling one of those ultrafake "I'm being celibate right now" rituals that women often pull to avoid the act. I was merely "preserving" myself to reach a higher level of sexual awareness. I didn't normally have to deal with dry spells, and on the rare instances when I did, I was well aware that a woman like Lynn could be incredibly dangerous. While she was busy working her magic, I'd be trying (most likely in vain) to maintain control. And when I totally lost it, she wouldn't be anywhere close to satisfaction. And unlike the many women who'd mastered the fine art of faking it in the name of allowing the man some sense of emotional pride and physical accomplishment, my ability to fake it and continue on would be nonexistent and she'd know it.

Then again, maybe she wouldn't.

Especially since she was fast asleep.

I sighed and slid onto the bed, beside her. My date was now a full-fledged failure. I hadn't stuck to my official nineteen-point date strategy. In fact, I'd handled my business so poorly that my plan never even got off the ground. Point one was simple: Turn off the telephone. I hadn't even managed to pull that off. And the fact that it was once again ringing, spoke volumes about what a loser I'd become.

"Hello," I said, picking up the receiver.

"Hey, Stu," Simon whispered. "When should I take the salad out of the fridge?"

"Why are you whispering, Simon?" I asked, frustrated. "Is Eve already there?"

"Nah, but it's already eight, so she should be here soon," he answered. "I saw how Lynn rushed you off the phone earlier, so I'm whispering so she won't sweat you."

"She's not sweating me now," I admitted, looking over at her.

"Is she still in the living room?"

"No," I remarked. "We're in the bedroom."

"Damn," he said, impressed. "You don't waste time, do you, money?"

"Oh no," I answered, lying. "I hit the jackpot. I told her about the trip and before I knew it, we rolled into the bedroom."

"So what's she doing while you're on the line?"

"She's knocked out."

"It's like that, Stu? You put old girl to sleep?"

"All I have to do is tuck her in," I replied, pulling a sheet up to her waist.

"I don't care what Rod and Trevor say—you're the man!" he exclaimed.

"Yeah," I sighed. "I'm the man alright."

"Stuart," Lynn whispered, yawning and reaching for my arm. "You were great."

"Touchdown!" Simon yelled, excited. "You must have blown her mind!"

"I have to go, sir," I said quickly. "And for the record, I believe salad is best served at room temperature."

"Who was that?" she asked, groggily.

"It was some guy from 'Who Wants To Be A Millionaire'," I lied.

"Are you going to be on?" she said, starting to sit up and reaching for her clothes.

"As soon as we get back from the trip," I commented, making one last attempt to make this evening a success.

"I thought the trip was great," she replied, slowly coming back to form. "It was, wasn't it?"

"Yeah," I sighed, helping her with her zipper. "It was—"

Before I could finish, she kissed me. And while our tongues raced around each other's mouths, my mind quickly clouded in thought. *I mentioned the trip and as far as I can tell, she hasn't turned me down... The champagne might have been doing the talking, but she thinks we've already been on a trip and she thought it was great—that's a good thing, isn't it?... I hope Simon gets that salad out of the fridge before Eve gets there.*

More than anything, I knew next time I was going with a trim and tidy three-item date list:

1. Mention the trip.
2. Sex.
3. Sign trip contract and insist on a nonrefundable deposit.

That was the only way things would work. Time was running short and I wasn't about to let Rod down. We couldn't possibly stand another useless evening like tonight. Even if it did end on a high note.

Maybe the night's not a total loss, I reasoned as her arms slid out of mine. *Girlfriend still kisses like a queen.*

Alan Jumps into
the Picture

Eighteen Minutes Later

Simon

S tuart was too lucky. He was a genius when it came to
women. He'd made his move, rocked Lynn to sleep
and would most likely have her carrying *his* bags on
the trip. Now it was my turn. If I knew Stuart, he had
played it fast and loose. He just opened the door, invited
her in and let the mood make itself. The food was perfect,
the wine was chilled to perfection and she probably ate the
dessert off of his stomach when they rolled into the bedroom. That's how it worked for Stuart when he was focused.

But me. I was in trouble.

While I sincerely appreciated Rod's dilemma and would love to have Eve on the trip, I had bigger fish to fry. Christmas was right around the corner and unlike Thanksgiving, spending it alone simply wasn't an option. I wanted to be somewhere with Eve. I wanted to be with her on the trip during New Year's Eve and to shower her with roses and flowers on Valentine's Day. She was special and I wanted her to know that.

Maybe it sounded crazy, but sometimes a woman came into your life who forced you to stop, if only for a second. With her, you saw why relationships could lift your spirit and bring out all the good that you had to offer. She helped you to see the value of communication and of late-into-the-night phone calls about nothing. You knew that with her, your life could be dramatically different and ultimately rewarding in ways you'd otherwise never realize.

And the beauty of it was that she helped you to feel all of this without ever really trying.

That's how I saw Eve. Our past, in all of its brevity, was the very best past I'd ever had with a woman. She made me feel more alive than the doctor who slapped at my tail when I was pulled out of my mother's womb. We talked about art, music, football and even relationships with an ease I'd been unable to find with any other woman. She was by far, the one woman who would cause me to break it off with another woman if she strolled back into my life.

Every guy had a woman like that. You daydreamed about how great things would be had you not blown it with her. She could call, say she was in town overnight and that she'd love to see you, and you'd drop whatever or *whomever* was the center of your attention. She wasn't the long-lost sweetheart who intimidated your wife at your high school reunion. She was that "other woman" whom neither the sweetheart or your wife knew about. We all had that woman. And because we'd either settled in for a suitable replacement or we shuddered at the financial and emotional toll of divorce, we hung in there and reminisced about our glorious past with our real Ms. Right.

As far as I could tell, Eve was my Ms. Right. And if I let that doorbell buzz much longer, she might turn around and leave before I could tell her.

"I'll be there in a second," I said, stuffing a newspaper beneath my couch.

I walked toward the door and sprayed a can of Glade air freshener before rolling it under the couch, where it landed beside the newspaper. The maid service wasn't available, so my choices were limited. This date was not getting off to a great start. But Stuart had all but supplied me with a restaurant-quality gourmet meal. All I had to do was present it without dropping any on her outfit, and the stage would be set. She'd jump into my life and onto that trip.

"Hi, Simon," she said, walking in. "Whew," she commented. "You went a little heavy on the air freshener didn't you?"

"Haven't you ever heard of setting the mood?" I asked, closing the door.

"The mood for what?" she replied, her hand waving in front of her face. "A trip to the bathroom?"

"It's nice to see you too," I answered, grinning.

"So why am I here?" she asked, taking a seat on the couch.

"You have to ask yourself that," I told her, reaching for a glass.

"Okay," she said, crossing her legs. "Why did you ask me over?"

"Why did you accept?"

"Because I figured you would give me some tips on my golf game," she laughed.

"Great," I replied, placing a glass on the coffee table in front of her. "What are you drinking tonight?"

"I'll pass," she answered.

"So how did your meeting go?"

"It went," she sighed. "Actually it was kind of boring," she remarked. "You know how it is with accountants and brokers. Everything's about the bottom line."

"Did I ever tell you about my buddy who's a broker?"

"If it's okay by you, I'd rather not talk business," she warned.

"Fine," I said, handing her a flaky, warm minicroissant. "No business," I added. "Just pleasure."

"Pleasure works for me," she remarked. "Hey," she noticed. "Something smells delicious. Did you cook?"

"It's probably the air freshener you just clowned me about," I joked, heading toward the kitchen. "But it just so happens that you're about to have a meal that's fit for a queen."

"I'll be the judge of that," she said, following me.

And judge she did. Eve and I had eaten out many times. But I'd never seen her light into food like tonight. Stuart wasn't just a cook. He was a chef. His lobster ravioli was superb and Eve loved it. The salad was light and tasty and Eve devoured it. And the sweet-potato cheesecake blew her mind as much as it blew mine. I immediately realized how he had landed Lynn in the bed and knew she was all but booked for the trip. And the door was now wide open for me. All I had to do was walk in and claim my prize.

"You are too much, Simon," she said, raising a glass of water to toast. "If I knew you could cook like this, I would have scooped you up and married you years ago."

"Are you serious?" I asked, excited.

"Of course," she answered. "Haven't you ever heard that the way to a woman's heart is through her stomach?"

"I've heard something like that," I told her. "But I never took you for the eating type."

"I love to eat," she confessed. "And I also love to cook."

"So how come I've never had the pleasure."

"You never asked."

"You've never let me close to your place," I reminded her. "To this day, I still don't know where you live."

"I never asked you over because I don't know you that well."

"We've known each other for years."

"True," she replied, sipping some water. "But coming over here was easier," she commented. "We both knew what was going to happen and that took away the pressure," she added. "If I would have invited you over, you might have gotten the wrong idea and I'm not interested in any drama."

And she wouldn't have gotten any from me. Even if she was wrong. It wasn't easier for men to entertain. If anything, it was tougher. When a guy visited a woman, he wasn't making an inventory of her household and belongings. He didn't inspect the window dressings or the color of the couch as it related to carpeting. And he could care less about the brand name worthiness of her appliances and accessories. If she had a master suite with a super bath, it mattered little. And additions like sunrooms, family rooms and powder rooms didn't move us.

If the food worked, we were okay. And since our visit was far from a final, premarital qualifier, the only thing we concerned ourselves with was the size of the TV screen and the quality of the cable television system. If the sports channels were grouped together, the woman's stature significantly increased. And if the porno channels were grouped together and were in relative proximity to the aforementioned sports channels, her relationship potential quotient was greatly enhanced.

It was different for guys. Simple visits were in reality complex evaluations. Women were attracted to men with potential. And simply put, your place and how you took care of it cut to the core of your potential. If you took care of your place, that special woman reasoned you had the potential to take care of her. And if your closets and kitchen cabinets were in order, it stood to reason that you conducted your affairs in an orderly fashion. Women had the upper hand when it came to knowing what to look for and they used it. And when it came to entertaining in general, the rules totally benefited them.

If you invited a lady over and decided to answer the door in say, a thong, what would happen? She'd probably have you arrested. But if you showed up at that same woman's home and *she* answered the door wearing little else than a thong—what would happen? You knew the drill. You grabbed the protection, you scooted to the bedroom and you prayed that she had cable when you were done.

The fact that women could literally decide the fate of an evening before the date ever got started spoke to the upper hand they'd been dealt when it came to entertaining. If you didn't, at a minimum, engage in some *useless* conversation, set out some *useless* food and jump through hoops to provide some *useless* form of atmosphere and entertainment, you'd be labeled as anything from cheap to unsophisticated to petty and downright scandalous.

And the food and other date-enabling items were *useless*, because in the final analysis, they were of little consequence. Did you think a few of those ridiculous dough-covered finger franks or some sappy buffalo-style wingettes would really sway a woman's opinion or actions? If she hated them, but already knew she was wearing that plastered-on miniskirt for a reason, those wings could grow feathers and fly around the room and she wouldn't even notice. And if she loved your stupid spinach balls, but was more interested in closing the blinds in your bedroom in the first place, the spinach balls would stay stuck on the tray, unless they grew legs and walked off. The decision to bed you down was made long before she hit the door and there was a possibility it was made by committee.

"Quit playing and give the man some," her girlfriend would tell her.

"And you better call us as soon as you get back home," another would say.

"But what if I'm not ready?" your date might respond to her girlfriend.

"You'd better get ready before *I* do," the first friend would warn.

Eve was off point. Men definitely had a tougher road to hoe when it came to entertaining. But I wasn't about to throw it in her face. At least not until I found where she stood on a relationship and I got her booked for the trip.

"Okay, Eve," I said, lighting a candle and sitting across from her. "You're right. I invited you over for a reason."

"I figured that," she said seductively. "But what if I had something else in mind?"

"Something like what?"

"Let's talk," she said.

"That's exactly what I had in mind," I told her.

"Shoot," she replied, smiling.

"Tell me about your family."

"What is it with my family?"

"You just said you wanted to talk," I reminded her. "And since I fed you like a queen *and* her army, I'll choose the topics."

"You know I don't like talking about my family," she warned. "But you asked, so here goes."

I didn't know what she would say, but I prepared myself for the worst. She'd never before agreed to talk about her past. I guessed she was from D.C., but for all I knew, she could have been the sister from another planet. I figured her firmly held secrecy was tied to just that, some big secret. It didn't help that the flickering candlelight allowed her to talk without ever having to look me in the eye. When you couldn't see a woman's eyes, you simply didn't know what you were about to get.

"I know what you're expecting," she started. "You're

thinking, 'ex-stripper, screwed-up background, incest, the whole nine,' but it's nothing like that. My parents were a happily married suburban couple and I was their well-adjusted, high-achieving, middle-class princess," she said. "I didn't kiss a boy until eighth grade and I held on to my virginity until I was eighteen," she bragged. "I wanted to marry my high school sweetheart and would have, if he hadn't died on me."

"He died?" I asked, surprised. "How old was he?"

"He passed on my twentieth birthday."

"What happened?"

"He OD'd," she told me. "He was strung out on heroin and he got his hands on a bad batch," she confided. "I'd done everything I could," she said, her voice starting to crack. "But at the funeral I realized I all but killed him."

"You weren't his dealer were you?" I asked, surprised.

"Of course not," she answered. "I was an enabler," she remarked. "I truly loved him and when I saw how much he needed the drugs, I wanted to give him everything I could."

"Let me guess. You got into dancing so he could support his habit."

"In a sense, yes," she replied. "But with me, it was more about control."

"Control?"

"When I saw how much my body could control what men did and how they thought, I was sold," she told me. "If I dressed supersexy, I could take a man's mortgage, his car-note and his and *my* grocery money in less than an hour," she shared. "And when I played it down, I could convince that same man and his half-drunken buddies to keep their money and go home to their wives and families."

"Did you ever feel guilty?"

"I wasn't a lawyer, I was a dancer," she laughed. "I danced because I wanted to dance," she confessed. "But I'd be lying if I said Alan didn't have something to do with it."

"Alan?"

"He was my boyfriend," she told me. "And when I found out he was hooked, I did everything I could to help," she went on. "We went to every twelve-step program we could find, I got him in five different rehabs, we went to meetings, I even used some of my dancing money to pay his dealer off so he wouldn't take Alan's calls," she admitted. "But when he confessed that he was a junkie he said that besides loving me, shooting-up was the only thing he lived for," she continued. "I didn't know what to do, but he was my man and I was going to take care of him, so I decided to use the only thing I had," she said sadly. "I used my body."

"I know this is going to sound corny, but you had your mind," I interrupted. "You could have used that."

"I did," she asserted. "My mind was on my man and how I could keep him safe and happy," she said, her head nodding. "I took control of the situation. He never wanted for a thing. And when he wasn't high and didn't have to worry where his next hit was coming from, he was an angel."

"I don't know that I've ever heard of a smack-shooting angel," I said, shaking my head in disbelief.

"You didn't know Alan," she said, wistfully. "He was

different, Simon," she started. "He never judged me and before he got hooked, he worked and took care of me like I was a prize," she told me. "I was in school, and he paid my tuition. I needed books and he bought every last one of them. And when I got sick, you would have sworn he was a certified MD," she added, softly weeping into a napkin. "I loved him with all my heart and soul," she continued. "And when he left, he took a part of me with him."

"So where do your parents play into this?" I asked, peering through the candlelight. "Why didn't they cover your tuition?"

"When they met Alan, they freaked out. They told me he'd ruin my life and they insisted that I stop seeing him," she remarked. "I wasn't having it. And their ultimatums didn't scare me, in fact, they just made me angry," she added. "So I moved out and Alan and I got an apartment in the city."

"Why did they have a problem with him. Was he old or something?"

"You got it," she answered. "And I'm sure the fact that he was old *and* white didn't help either."

"Your mind is all screwed-up over some dead, old white guy?" I asked, surprised.

"He was the love of my life," she quickly replied. "And last time I checked, my mind wasn't at all screwed-up," she said, with an edge.

"I didn't mean it like that," I replied, not wanting any tension. "I'm just kind of surprised," I told her. "I would have never expected—"

"You wouldn't have expected what?" she interrupted. "That I'm capable of love?" she added. "If you ever get lucky enough to find love, I hope you run after it, Simon," she insisted. "If you won't fight for it like a junkyard dog and if you're not willing to take the risk of getting hurt to get what you really want, you're a chump," she told me. "And the only one you've cheated is yourself," she added. "If you've never wanted a woman to be even happier than you and if you don't know how it feels to care about some-one more than life itself, you probably don't understand what I'm saying," she reasoned. "I just hope you're smart enough to look at her heart, her eyes and her soul," she continued. "If you're so shallow that you'd allow the color of someone's skin to interfere with your happiness, then I truly feel sorry for you," she went on. "Because you'll miss out on the single greatest feeling any human can know," she said, staring me in the eye.

"And what's that, Eve?" I asked, almost certain of her answer.

"You'll miss out on love."

chapter 18

Tyra Goes Topsy-Turvy

Two Days Later

Simon

Nowhere.

That's exactly where I'd gotten with Eve the other night. Nowhere. We held hands and even hugged for a few uneasy moments, but she "discovered" she had to leave and suddenly was out the door even quicker than she'd come in. After what she'd said about Alan, I wanted to know even more. Like, did he know he'd turned her toward stripping? Did she actually prefer old white guys over young, fat black guys like me? And more important, did she think she'd ever position herself to fall in love again? I wanted to know all of that and so much more. But she wasn't having it. I'd known Eve, in some form or fashion, for nearly ten years. And with one ten-minute conversation, I'd picked up more about her and how she saw herself and the world around her than I'd learned in that decade.

Besides the tales of drugs, dancing and commitment beyond the call of duty, what stuck with me most was her well-received warning. I've replayed it over and over in my head, like a worn-out CD: *"If you ever get lucky enough to find love, I hope you run after it, Simon. If you won't fight for it like a junkyard dog and if you're not willing to take the risk of getting hurt to get what you really want, you're a chump. And the only one you've cheated is yourself."*

She was right. I was a chump's chump. There was no way I should have let her out that door without at least making an attempt to tell her what I was thinking. All I wanted was half a chance. I knew that with the slightest of chances, Eve and I could have a warm and relevant relationship. But I didn't take the chance and much like she said, the only person I cheated was myself. Stuart at least had the guts to take a risk. He put it on the line. And he was only looking for a date. I wanted even more, and all I'd come up with was "I'm glad you liked the cheesecake." If that was putting it on the line, I'd never get anywhere.

Besides where I was right then.

Stuart called with an idea and suggested that we meet at Georgetown Park Mall in the city. Though I wasn't exactly

interested in running the malls with him, he convinced
me to take the day off in the name of Christmas shopping.
It was a Friday, and the thought of a long weekend didn't
seem too bad, so I called in sick. It didn't hurt that Stuart
bragged about an idea that he said could seal the deal with
Eve. I almost ran to the driveway butt-naked when he uttered the magic words, "When you pull this off, Eve will
probably get herself a pilot's license and fly all of us over
to Cancun." The trip had lost its luster for me. I wanted
more. And after the other night, I'd promised myself that
she was going to know how I felt the very next time I saw
her. But Rod's situation added a sense of urgency. Even if
I didn't want to make the trip, Rod's dilemma sealed it. I
was going and Eve would be right there with me.

"My man, Simon," Stuart said, spotting me as I walked
into the mall.

"What's up, Stu?" I casually asked, reaching to shake his
hand.

"Where's the Christmas spirit?" he asked, smiling
broadly.

"It walked out of my front door two nights ago," I answered, referring to Eve.

"Well lighten up, my friend," he said, grabbing my
arm. "It walked into my door and our fates have changed."

"What do you mean, 'our' fates?"

"You remember when you called last night?" he started.

"Yeah," I answered. "You had just hit her with the crab
balls."

"Is food your frame of reference for everything?" he
asked, sounding disgusted. "I'm talking about when we
were in the bedroom."

"And she was eating the sweet-potato cheesecake off of your stomach?"

"Can I get some help over here!" he yelled. "Somebody from 'I Can't Stop Thinking About Food' Anonymous or something?" he added. "She wasn't eating off my stomach," he told me. "In fact," he finished. "She was knocked out."

"Truth be told, that cheesecake is so rich it puts me to sleep too," I confessed.

"I can't be having this conversation," he muttered, upset. "Simon," he said, shaking me. "Lynn and I didn't sleep together," he insisted. "She got *tipsy*," he said, sarcastically, "and it was lights out before I could even make a move."

"So you're saying—"

"You got it," he interrupted. "No action with her and even less action on the trip," he confided. "But I was watching some flick last night," he added, now smiling. "And the answer to our prayers was revealed."

"Look, Stu," I said, shaking my head in disappointment. "I don't even know where to buy rooffies and even if I did, I wouldn't want to roll like that."

"Simon," he demanded. "Shut up and follow me."

We headed down an escalator and then walked toward one of my favorite places, Victoria's Secret. I'd long marveled at their catalogs and their Super Bowl commercials. I don't know a guy who hasn't fantasized about making it with one of their models on some hot beach. And when it struck me that Cancun was some hot beach, I immediately wanted to know what he had in mind.

"You remember telling me how hard it is to talk to Eve?" Stuart asked, standing at the store's entrance.

"I've had more success talking to walls," I admitted.

"Well, in this movie, the guy wanted to take his lady skiing, so he gave her a tiny box of snow," he told me.

"I know we didn't come here to buy a box of sand," I remarked. "And how did he give her a box of snow without it melting anyway?" I asked.

"He took her to some restaurant, and he asked the hostess to hold it in the ice box."

"Oh, I get it," I said sarcastically. "I'm supposed to take Eve to a pet shop and ask *their hostess* to hold my *sand* in the snake pit," I went on. "And the python will bite my hand off when I go to get the box, then you can take Eve to Cancun for me," I added. "We'd be better off with the rooffies," I reasoned.

"I'd die before I'd get caught somewhere with Eve," he answered, laughing. "But if she keeps her nose clean, I'll ask Lynn to give her some pointers."

"Why are we standing in front of this store?" I asked, hoping to change the topic.

"We're going to use the same move as the guy in the movie," he said, walking in.

"Last time I checked, they didn't sell snow at Victoria's Secret."

"Since we're not looking for snow, that won't be a problem," he answered, flagging down a salesperson.

I'd heard that locating a sales rep in a superbusy store like Victoria's Secret was nearly impossible during the holiday season. But no one ever told me finding one who was as beautiful as any one of their catalog models would be quite this easy. As she walked toward us, I imagined her shiny jet-black hair blowing gently in an island breeze.

She was wearing one of those super-tiny string bikinis, and smiled at me as she drew closer. All we needed was sun, an umbrella and a gallon of sunscreen to finish the deal. But first she'd lean over and whisper, "Can I—"

"...help you, sir?" she asked.

I stood in complete silence. Still thinking she was going to ask to rub sunscreen on me. But it wasn't happening. Especially since Stuart was nudging me in the side.

"Simon," he whispered. "She asked if she could help you."

"Hell yeah, she can help," I answered, still in a daze. "She can help with anything she wants."

"I'm Candi," she cheerily stated. "I'll be your lingerie service technician, and I'd be happy to help you find something for that special lady," she said, sounding more like a spokesperson for the National Association of Helium Lovers.

"Well, we have a major problem and we need some help quick," Stuart remarked.

"Can you explain this lingerie service technician deal?" I asked, joking. "Do you like come out and fix a teddy in case something goes wrong?"

"I don't know if we do that, but I can ask one of our senior lingerie service technicians if you'd like," she replied, sounding as lost as I usually feel on a first date.

"Why don't we skip that part for right now?" Stuart asked, smiling. "We know what we're looking for and something tells me you're one of the very best lingerie service technicians in the business."

"You can tell already?" she answered, grinning. "This is only my first day."

"We're looking for two bikinis," Stuart shared.

"And which one of you will be wearing them?" she asked. "Because the plus-size section is on the other side of the store," she added, smiling at me.

"Actually, we're looking for two lady friends of ours," Stuart told her. "Instead of Christmas in July, we're doing a July in Christmas thing."

"Nobody told me they moved it to July," she said clumsily. "There goes white Christmas," she said, giggling.

"Now I know where I know you from!" I exclaimed. "You're one of those twins. You're Topsy!"

"Not quite," she answered, embarrassed. "I'm Turvy. My sister is Topsy, but she works night shift."

"Am I missing something here?" Stuart asked, concerned.

"The Topsy-Turvy twins!" I exclaimed. "They do the 'good manners' segment on that afternoon kids' show," I told him. "Topsy says this and Turvy says that," I said, putting on a bad impersonation. "Every little boy worth his salt watches it."

"Oh," Stuart commented, his head nodding. "*Those* Topsy-Turvy twins," he remarked. "The ones with the poster and the website."

"Is it okay to call you Turvy?" I asked, smiling broadly.

"I guess so," she answered, popping on some bubblegum.

"So Turvy," Stuart started. "If I wanted to take you to an exotic beach and I gave you a bikini as a hint to my intentions, would that piss you off?"

"It depends," she responded.

"On what?" I asked, unable to budge the smile off my face.

"On whether or not you gave me a thong," she told us.

"So a thong is the wrong way to go, huh?" Stuart asked her.

"No way," she answered, smiling. "If you gave me a thong, at least I'd know your intentions before I said yes."

"I think I just fell in love," I muttered.

"If you tell me about your friends, maybe I can help you," she told us. "Duh," she added, surprising us. "We have this new feature that's totally awesome," she shared, sounding excited. "Do your friends shop here?"

"Mine does," Stuart quickly answered.

"And what about yours?" she asked, turning toward me. "I think I told you we have a plus-size department on the other side."

"That you did," I answered. "But she's not what you call *plus size,*" I whispered.

"Come over here and I'll get you started," she said, leading us toward two computers.

"Why can't we just give you their names?" I asked, following her.

"It's no fun that way," she answered, pulling out my chair. "We'll tell you who she is based on what you tell us about her," she added. "And you wouldn't want to miss the presentation," she said, grinning. "I hear all the guys like it."

"It sounds like you all have built up quite the little database," Stuart remarked, trying to flirt.

"After we figure out her name, we can even tell you if some other guy bought her something," she teased. "But I'm a good lingerie service technician and a good lingerie service technician would never do that."

"That won't be a problem here," Stuart bragged. "If

somebody else even thinks about buying her a bikini, I'll kill him."

"Just fill out the questionnaire on the screen, and we'll narrow things down by their bra sizes," she told us. "And then we can tell you what they like," she added, moving the mouse to restart the computers. "Do you guys know their bra sizes?"

"Of course," I answered, smiling.

"Super," she answered. "Does your friend have a website too?"

"Excuse me?" Stuart asked.

"Guys know my bra size because it's on my website," she casually remarked. "So I just figured your friend had a website too."

She figured wrong. Any guy with half a brain knew a woman's bra size long before she ever let on. Some guys were just plain bold. Give them one phone call, and they'd get a woman to share her measurements as if they were a condition of employment. I was certain many a call had ended with some dim-witted guy spouting out, "Sorry, sweetheart, but a 36-B just won't cut it. I'm actually in the market for 36-C."

Men used a wide variety of creative measures to elicit a woman's bra size or her measurements. Most guys believed if you could even get a woman to discuss the topic, it was the gateway to other more substantial subjects like sex, her tendencies in regard to affection and her attitudes toward ménages à trois and one-night stands. As far as men were concerned, a woman who bragged, "I'm a 38-D and proud of it," was more likely to be open to new and exciting sexual challenges. Why else would she be proud of her 38-Ds?

It was like a guy with big biceps. Did you think he worked out so that those sculpted arms would fill out his shirt-sleeves? No way. He did it because lots of women found it attractive. And just like Ms. 38-D, he was down for whatever.

If a woman refused to discuss her bra size, you knew your work was cut out for you. She might turn out to be a real zinger in bed, but most guys believed she'd be quite the opposite. "If she's not giving up the bra size," a seasoned guy would reason, "she'll be giving out more orders than an army colonel in bed." Instead of you saying, "Whose stuff is this?" she'd say to you, 'Tell me who's the woman! Tell me I'm the one!' "

You knew if she kept her measurements out of the discussion, you'd have to work quickly when your shot came. One night after lovemaking she'd mosey off to the bathroom or the kitchen and her bra would lay on the floor just waiting for you to make your move. You'd think you'd stumbled onto a gold mine and would waste little time retrieving your prize, locating the label and committing that bra size to memory. *What's the equivalent of a Wonderbra for men?... If she's wearing a 36-D, I'm packing eight inches easy...I hope I can find the size and get to sleep before she gets back.*

Turvy was wrong. But that was okay. I cut her some slack because she looked like a *real* 36-D. I'd been to her website. I knew.

"Let's just say that we know," Stuart and I said together.

"Great," she told us. "We separate our clientele by their bra sizes."

"A guy had to come up with that," I commented, reaching over to slap Stuart five.

"My lady's a firm 34-C," Stuart admitted.

"So is Eve," I chimed in.

"I'll just let you guys fill out your surveys," she told us. "Just answer what you can and I'll set up your presentations," she said, walking away.

What immediately struck me was how little I knew about Eve. The questions were simple and I knew some of the answers—the color, make and model of her car, her occupation and where she worked— those were easy. But I was missing out on the key elements that made her who she was. Her religion? Her political affiliation? . . . Her favorite book? . . . Her personal inspiration? Her idea of a romantic evening . . . Her fantasies . . . Her dreams . . .

The answers weren't coming as fast as I wanted. And sadly, Stuart seemed to be having the same problem.

"Simon," he started, bending to see my screen. "What am I supposed to say? I don't know all of this stuff."

"*You* don't know all of it?" I asked, frustrated. "I couldn't even fill in the address part," I added. "And how am I supposed to know if she uses soap or shower gel?"

"Tell me about it," he commented. "I know where Lynn went to school because we took a class together."

"I know where Eve works," I confessed, embarrassed. "And I know she went to school, but I don't know where," I went on. "It actually came up the other night, but I didn't get the details."

"It sounds like you should have taken the chance," Turvy said, approaching us. "Women really like it when you ask them stuff."

"I'll have to remember that," Stuart replied, submitting a few final answers to the questionnaire.

"All you have to do is hit ENTER and we'll have an answer in just a second," she said, opening a set of black drapes.

I wasn't sure what was going to happen next, but I was willing to run with it. She turned our chairs around to reveal twin television monitors and said to us, "Sit tight for your *presentation*. You guys are in for a big surprise."

Bring it on, I thought, recalling the bikini shots on her website.

"The results are in," she boasted, now standing in front of us. "And you're not going to believe this," she said, smiling. "But you guys are dating the same woman!" she exclaimed. "How wild is that?"

"If we were dating the same woman don't you think we'd know it?" I asked, unimpressed.

"Yeah," Stuart chimed in. "Your computer program must be wrong," he reasoned. "There's no way Lynn would date somebody like him."

"What's that supposed to mean?" I asked, offended.

"You're not her type," he remarked. "And you're my man, so you know that's nothing against you," he told me. "Lynn's one of those frilly wine and cheese babes," he continued. "You know the type. If you're not wearing a white collar and driving a high-end sports car, she's not interested," he shared. "She's ballet and theater. That's why I was so surprised to see her at D & B's," he finished. "It's just not her style."

"I know what you mean," I said, nodding in agreement. "I can't see Eve swinging with a guy like you," I told him. "She's not into all that style over substance nonsense," I remarked. "She's one of those independent types who likes to kick back, chill and check out some videos," I

Van Whitfield

added. "She doesn't trip off of that white collar pomp and circumstance because she has to deal with it all day at the job," I went on. "And after ten minutes with me, there's no way she'd roll with you."

"Okay, Mr. Ego-heads," Turvy interrupted. "It says right here that you're dating the same woman and she just happens to be here."

She then closed the curtains behind us and stepped to the side.

"Don't fight over her," she said, dimming the lights. "Meet Ms. Tyra Banks," she said cheerfully. "Or as we call her," she finished. "*Cyber*-Tyra!"

The screens glowed and the show started. In front of us was a true to life presentation of the woman we both *wanted* to date. Tyra paraded across the screen in a beautiful metallic bikini and then turned as if she were smiling at both of us. Then the real show started. Two full-size Tyra-holograms appeared in front of us and danced to Lil' Kim's old-school anthem, "Crush on You." And when the late, great Notorious B.I.G. hit the chorus, "I know you seen me on the video," Stuart and I quickly chimed in, "True," as if he was in front of us alongside Cyber-Tyra.

"Is this what you'd like me to wear in Cancun?" Stuart's Tyra asked, smiling.

"I can wear this to the beach or to the Jacuzzi," mine seductively told me.

"Or do you like this better?" Stuart's Tyra asked, spinning around to reveal a leopard-spotted thong set.

"I think we're ready for the same type of action," my Tyra naughtily whispered, turning to share a tiger-striped thong ensemble.

She then moved to fulfill my wildest of dreams. Her hands crept upward and she slowly started to open her top and share with me the singular sight that men the world over had anticipated for the last five years. I was about to see what made her bra proud.

At least I thought I was about to see them.

As soon as she moved to spread her top apart, the lights zoomed on and the show was over. Unlike me, Stuart was all smiles. His Cyber-Tyra was doing the same thing as mine. But he'd seen more than enough. For an instant, he was actually happy that we were dating the same woman. That didn't work for me. I'd never before been that close to perfection. Even if it was a life-sized hologram that was tied to some tiny computer chip.

"Can you bring her back?" I asked pathetically. "She was about to take her top off."

"It's okay," Turvy said, walking in. "I hear they're implants."

"I don't think that matters," Stuart and I acknowledged together.

"Well," she said, reading from a tiny note card. "The results are in and I think you're in for a surprise," she told us. "I'm glad you're sitting down."

"Technology is incredible," Stuart commented, still smiling. "Can you believe it, Simon?" he added. "All we had to do was fill out a form and now she's going to tell us what our lady friends like."

"Not exactly," she interrupted.

"So what exactly are you going to tell us?" I asked, thinking back to Cyber-Tyra and her tiger-striped thong.

"I don't know how to say this," she started. "But you're dating the same woman."

"We know!" we yelled, excited. "We're dating Tyra Banks!"

"I wouldn't be so excited," some gray-haired older woman remarked, poking her head in the curtains. "I hear they're implants."

"It doesn't matter!" we happily answered.

"Does the name Evelyn Chambers ring a bell?" Turvy asked, bringing us back to reality.

"Of course it does," Stuart started. "I told you this technology jazz was the ticket," he added. "You see what they did there, Simon?" he asked, smiling. "I barely gave them anything and they came back with Lynn's name."

"That's funny," I told them, stunned. "She has the same name as Eve."

"That's because she *is* Eve," Turvy commented.

"Yeah, I know," I joked. "We're dating Tyra Banks too," I said, grinning. "Remember?"

"Does Tyra Banks work at Strawn, Levinson and Blume?" she asked.

"That's where Lynn works," Stuart said, worried.

"It's where Eve works too," Turvy shared. "She also drives a—"

"Midnight black—" I said, jumping in.

"Lexus sports coupe—" Stuart interrupted.

"Evelyn Chambers," I muttered, concerned. "Eve . . ."

"Lynn . . ." Stuart, nervously added.

"—Chambers," Turvy finished, gloating. "You guys are best friends and you didn't even know?" she asked. "And they call me kooky?"

We slowly looked at each other and thought the worst of thoughts. If Evelyn Chambers was indeed Eve Chambers *and* Lynn Chambers, somebody was in trouble. But who?

Dating a woman your friend once went out with was like a bad dream. Dating a woman your friend had *slept with* was a full-blown nightmare. You'd probably had long discussions about your buddy and didn't even know it. And worse than that, they'd probably laughed about you without *your* knowing it. Did she do the same things with you *and* to you that she did with him? Did she call him when she couldn't reach you? Did she fantasize about threesomes with you and your buddy like you fantasized about threesomes with her and friends? Did that very same friend of hers know that she was playing both you and your buddy? And what if your girl—your buddy's girl didn't even know?

I couldn't figure it out. It made no sense. Eve was Lynn. Lynn was Eve. And Stuart and I were even more kooky than Turvy, and she put the "kook" in the word, even if she was a *real* 36-D. Rod wouldn't believe this and Trevor wouldn't let us live it down. With less than a week to book our tickets, we had played all our options. Or more to the point, our singular option had played *us*.

We didn't dare utter a word. I was certain neither of us knew what to say. But I knew exactly what Stuart was thinking, because my mind was stuck on the same ridiculous thought: *Where the hell is Cyber-Tyra when you need her?!*

chapter 19

Eve-Lynn and Evelyn Come Alive

Moments Later

Simon

tuart and I wasted little time getting out of the store. But not before Turvy foolishly asked, "Since you're buying for the same woman, maybe one of you could pay for the top while the other one buys the thong."

I wasn't about to buy Eve anything. And I bet Stuart felt the exact same way.

"Why are you trying to date my woman?" he asked, walking toward the food court, which was a few paces ahead of us.

"What do you mean *your* woman?" I fired back. "You

don't even want a woman, *Mr. 'I Have as Many Dates as I Have Shoes,'*" I commented. "And besides," I added, "I knew her before you did."

"That's precisely my point," he said, locating an empty table. "She started with you, but she wound up with me."

"Don't get beside yourself," I remarked, reaching for a seat. "She ended up with me the other night."

"But she ate *my* food."

"If you hadn't bored her to death when she was at your spot, she would've never made it to my place," I shot back.

"And had I known she was coming to your place, I would have *never* given you the food in the first place."

"Are you sure you didn't sleep with her?" I asked, concerned.

"If I did I wouldn't tell you," he quickly answered.

"You probably never hit it anyway," I commented.

"Then how do I know about the mole?"

"You know about the mole?" I asked, surprised.

Then I knew he and Eve had been together at some point. She called it her "little love mark." But like Stuart, I knew it was a mole. It sat at the very top of her thigh, less than a millimeter below the gateway to her G spot. She once boasted, "The only way a man gets to see my little love mark is to have his face in exactly the right spot. And the only way he'll see it is if his eyes are wide open when he's taking care of business."

Just thinking of it made me sick. Stuart had been with *my* Eve. He'd actually seen the mole. I didn't know why it was bugging me like this. It's not like he'd known. But why hadn't he? Why hadn't she told him about me? Why hadn't she told me about *him*? Did she think he was better in the sack? Did she prefer him roaming near her little love mark? Was he the guy she went out with the night we were almost robbed? And which one of us did she like the most?

I had to know.

"You know what you are, don't you?" I asked.

"What?"

"You're the other guy," I said, forcefully. "And everybody knows the woman never ends up with the other guy."

"I'm the other guy?" he huffed. "I'm the other guy?" he repeated, his voice rising. "Let's get this straight right now," he said, looking me in the eye. "The only *other guy* here is you."

"Are you guys arguing about the woman with the implants?" the gray-haired older woman from Victoria's Secret asked, passing by.

"I should have known you'd pull something like this," Stuart commented.

"*I* didn't do anything," I told him. "You didn't want her. All you wanted was a date for the trip."

"And you didn't?" he asked, upset.

"I could have cared less about that stupid trip," I confessed. "I wanted Eve straight-up," I admitted. "And you know it because I told you."

"Yeah," he replied, unimpressed. "But instead of telling me, you should have told *her*."

"You're right," I said, starting to stand. "I don't even know why I'm wasting my time with you," I added.

"Where are you going?" Stuart asked, surprised. "We haven't finished arguing."

"What are you, a housewife?" I remarked sarcastically.

"I'm heading down to her job so we can put an end to this crap."

"I don't think so, Simon," he said, rising to his feet. "You're not going without me."

"You *are* a housewife," I replied, heading toward the door. "But you're right. You should come. If you see me and Eve together, maybe you'll back off and find your own woman."

We waited at a taxi stand for just a few seconds and we were quickly whisked off to Eve's office at the venerable brokerage house of Strawn, Levinson and Blume. I'd never been to her office and didn't know what to expect or what I would say. I didn't want to be mad at Stuart, but I couldn't help it. And Stuart being Stuart didn't help.

"Do you realize you're not her type?" he asked, looking out the window.

"The only thing I realize is that you should shut the hell up," I answered.

"Women like Lynn don't hook up with guys like you, Simon. There's no way you're her type."

"Her name is *Eve,*" I reminded him. "And since I'm through discussing it with you, would you please shut your pie hole?"

"What do you think she's going to say? 'Oh, Simon, you're the man I've always wanted.' "

"We'll find out, won't we?" I remarked. "And that scares the hell out of you, doesn't it?" I asked. "You don't know how you're going to handle her telling you to take a hike because she'd rather be with your best friend."

"If you think she's going to say that, you're crazier than I thought," he told me.

"You don't know how crazy I am," I scowled. "And you don't want to see how crazy I can be."

"Excuse me, Mr. Crazy Man," the driver interrupted, with an accent as thick as my thighs. "But this lady. She is nice lady, no?"

"Yes," Stuart answered.

"She's very nice," I acknowledged.

"She can't be nice, no?" the driver commented, pulling to the curb in front of a sleek office building.

"What are you talking about?" I asked, reaching for the door.

"You say he is best friend, no?"

"You could say that," I slowly replied.

"*You* just say that, Mr. Crazy Man," he reminded me. "And nice woman not let best friend fight over nice woman, no?" he finished.

"No," Stuart somberly replied.

"You're right," I admitted. "She'd never go for that."

"Very good to know," the cabbie said, smiling. "You pay fare now."

"I'll let my *best friend* swing it," I said, opening the door and stepping onto the sidewalk.

I waited for Stuart as he argued over the tab.

"Advice worth five dollars!" I overheard the cabbie yell. "Best friend of Mr. Crazy Man is cheap!"

He was right. Stuart had money and he could be cheap. But he was my best friend. And I didn't want our friendship to be blown to bits because of *any* woman. Even one as sharp as Eve. We needed to bury the hatchet before we got to her. As I considered it, we needed to approach her with a game plan, much like a woman would. If a woman found her best friend had anything at all to do with a man she was involved with, she'd talk it out with her best friend and then cook up an elaborate scheme to catch him.

A lawyer buddy of mine, Eric, was living proof of such a scheme. He got jammed when he committed the single most heinous act of betrayal any woman can face.

He made a move with his lady's best friend.

His lady, Perri, lured him over one evening and had him strip down to his Skivvies. He thought he'd struck gold. She gave him "the full monty," and then bedded him down. She told him a water main break had hit the neighborhood, so he couldn't wash up before he left.

Eric then "crept" over to see her best friend, Lydia, who lived just a few blocks away and got the same treatment he'd received at Perri's. When he thought she was asleep, he slipped into his underwear and Lydia softly whispered, "Aren't you going to wash up?"

"I thought there was a water main break," Eric remarked.

"That was around the corner," she told him. "And how did you know about that?"

He worried he had been busted.

But Lydia let him off the hook and didn't ask another question.

"You can just take those off, grab a fresh pair from the drawer and hop in the shower before you leave," she insisted.

Eric was in heaven. He'd scored twice on the same night and would make it home to his *wife* freshly showered and with enough time to catch "SportsCenter" on ESPN. He *knew* he was the man.

What he didn't know was that he was about to get a front-and-center education on how quickly heaven can turn to hell, and on how the new millennium had produced a new and creative method for high-tech entrapment—"the DNA beat down."

Lydia wasted little time calling Perri, who had already had a conversation with Eric's wife—she had retrieved the number from Eric's Palm Pilot. Lydia and Perri had conspired to trap him. There hadn't been a water main break and Lydia had pretended to sleep, knowing Eric would climb into his underwear. She even scooped up his soiled pair of boxers while he showered. After all, she needed them for evidence.

But it didn't stop there.

Lydia and Perri knew a woman who specialized in identifying DNA samples for a celebrated D.C.-based PI. And on that very night, they took Eric's twice-stained underwear to her home-based lab and paid top dollar to get the goods on him. The test would prove Eric had been with both of them because their DNA would be firmly implanted in his underwear.

The next morning, while he showered for work, Lydia, Perri and Eric's wife convened in Eric's living room and hashed over the evidence and a lab report confirming his trysts.

When he saw them together as he walked downstairs, he passed out.

And when he awoke at the bottom of the stairs moments later, he literally saw the beginning of the end of his life.

The mighty triumvirate stood over him, Perri and

Lydia sipped on breakfast champagne cocktails and yelled, "Busted!" But his wife remained eerily calm. She didn't yell. She didn't cuss. She didn't even demand an explanation. "Get out and don't say a word," she said coldly. "And if you cross my door again, I'll have you killed while I'm spending *your* money on a cruise."

He got to his feet, headed toward the door and prepared for the worst. Which he got. Thanks to his indiscretions and Perri and Lydia's use of the DNA beat down, Eric was creamed in divorce court and his wife, ironically, hooked up with his best friend.

The worst act of betrayal any man can face.

We needed to trap Eve just like Perri and Lydia nailed Eric. And to my surprise, Stuart was thinking the same exact thing.

"We need to nail her," Stuart said, looking up at the building.

"What's the move?"

"How should I know?" he asked. "I've never been through this crap before."

"I have an idea," I remarked, walking toward the building. "Let's skip the games and get to the point."

"The point being?" he replied.

"The point is we have a trip and we both want the same woman to go," I started. "I know Eve and I seriously doubt that she knows what's going on," I confessed. "So we'll spill the beans and let her make the choice."

"You really like her, don't you?" he asked.

"Yeah," I sighed. "And I'm not about to play any games with her."

"What if she picks me?" he asked, sounding concerned.

"She won't."

"What makes you so sure?"

"You probably won't understand this, Stu, but we have a connection," I told him.

"If you're so connected, how did I get in the picture?"

"I never told her how I felt," I admitted.

"Maybe she didn't want to hear it," Stuart suggested.

"Maybe she didn't," I shared. "But I'm taking the ball out of her court. Before she decides on anything, she's going to know how I feel."

"What if she doesn't want either one of us?" he asked, worried.

"We'll bite the bullet and call Amber and Sonya from last year," I said, laughing.

"With our luck, some poor idiots probably married them," he said, now smiling. "Look, Simon, if you really think Eve is your Ms. Right, I'll back off," he told me.

"I don't want it that way," I answered. "I never want to wonder about what she would've done if she had the choice," I reasoned. "If she picks you, I'll have to live with it, and if I'm the one, at least I'll know the choice was hers."

That was the only way it could be. We walked in the building and headed toward the elevator. We didn't make it. Stuart insisted on taking a trip to the bathroom. He wanted to make sure he looked okay. I was less concerned about my look. My big interest was making sure my brain and my mouth were in synch with my heart. They had to be on the same page. When you put it all on the line, sounding like you had at least a little sense was a major plus.

And when I spotted her glancing at a newspaper and

walking across the lobby, everything went into overdrive. She wasn't just beautiful. She was the package. And I couldn't say anything to blow it. I had to be cool.

"Miss Chambers!" I yelled, waving across the lobby.

"Simon?" she answered, looking around. "What are you doing here?"

"We need to talk," I said, walking toward her.

"This sounds serious," she said, smiling. "Are you about to tell me I'm pregnant?"

"It *is* serious," I said, reaching for her hand. "There's something I think you should know."

"Are you okay?" she asked, concerned.

"That depends," I answered, showing her to the ledge of a huge potted ficus tree.

"On what?" she answered, starting to sit.

"On who you choose," I said, sitting down beside her.

"What are you talking about, Simon?"

"Forget I said that," I said, trying to stay focused. "Eve," I started. "How do you feel about me? And don't give me that 'you're a nice guy and I really enjoy your company' garbage."

"But I really do like you," she answered. "And I've always enjoyed your company."

"We're going to have to speed this up," I reasoned.

"Why?"

"Because someone's going to be here in just a few seconds and there's going to be a lot of explaining to do," I told her.

"I know you didn't bring one of those little hoochie mommas from your bus down to my job," she shot back.

"I don't drive a bus, Eve," I stressed. "I operate a vehicle," I added. "And she's not a hoochie momma. She's a he."

"Simon," she gasped, worried. "Did you come down here to tell me you're gay?"

"That's why I can't get a woman right now," quipped a frail, young-looking guy, sweeping the floor. "Why can't you gay guys stick with each other? There's nothing wrong with that."

"I'm not gay," I told him.

"Hey, Simon," Stuart said, approaching us. "You're right about working this thing out. We can't let Lynn come between us."

"I guess he's not gay either," the cleaning guy remarked, looking us over.

"Stuart?" Eve asked, surprised. "Wait a minute," she gasped, placing her hand over her heart. "You know Simon?"

"Open your eyes, sweetheart," the cleaning guy begged. "He doesn't just know him, he's his lover."

"He's not my lover," Stuart said, taken aback.

"I wouldn't claim his big behind either!" the cleaning guy exclaimed, walking away in disgust.

"What is this about?" Eve asked, sounding agitated. "What's going on here?"

"We need you to choose," I told her.

"And what is it that I'm choosing?" she snapped.

"Either me or him," I started. "I don't know if you realize it," I added. "But Stuart and I have been best friends since we were kids."

"You and Stuart?" she said, surprised. "But you're so different."

"So you're saying that you didn't know, right?" Stuart asked.

"Of course I didn't know," she answered, seeming a bit calmer. "How would I have known?"

"Great," Stuart said, jumping in. "So my solution will work here."

"What solution?" I asked.

"We can split her up," he suggested. "I'll take her on the trip and when we get back she's all yours."

"Are you crazy, Stuart?" I asked, upset.

"So you're saying you should take her on the trip and then I can have her?" he asked.

"You *are* crazy!" Eve told him. "I'm not a piece of property, and I'm not—"

"Eve," I interrupted. "You remember what you said the other night?" I asked.

"I said lots of things," she recalled.

"I'm talking about the part where you said if you think you've found that special person, you have to go for it," I reminded her.

"I said that?"

"You said you're a chump if you don't make a move."

"I said that too?" she repeated. "Was I drinking?"

"You did the drinking at my place," Stuart remarked. "You ate at his spot, but since it was *my* food, you technically were eating with me."

"It was your food?" she asked, surprised. "What kind of game are you two playing?"

"We're not playing anything," I asserted. "We didn't even know *you* were *you* until we went to Victoria's Secret."

"And what's with the different names?" Stuart quickly asked.

"What different names?" she replied. "My name is Evelyn," she said. "Some of my friends call me Eve and some call me Lynn," she told us. "You and I met three years ago, Stuart," she went on. "There were two Eves working at my firm, and I got tired of my ideas being passed over because the other Eve was always screwing up, so I told them to call me Lynn, and it stuck."

"So you prefer Eve?" I asked.

"I went back to it the same day the other Eve got fired," she stressed. "And I know who I am, so I don't get all bent out of shape when people who knew me as Lynn still call me Lynn," she said. "And since everybody's asking questions here," she finished, "how exactly does Victoria's Secret play into this?"

"Between the Tyra Banks hologram and your bra size, they tracked you right down," Stuart told her.

"Tyra Banks knows my bra size?" she asked, hurrying to cross her arms across her chest.

It didn't matter what Cyber-Tyra knew. This situation was getting us in deeper trouble with every sentence. A woman would never handle it this way. She'd get right to the point and have the most important question answered in minutes. "Who do you really want?" she'd ask. "Because if you want her, you need to step."

Guys didn't have that killer instinct. We didn't even know how to break up with women. We basically utilized one of two methods. You either made her break up with you or you just stopped participating by becoming more invisible than you already were. We didn't take rejection well, so we naturally thought women were much like us. Nobody liked hurting someone else's feelings. And guys foolishly reasoned that stringing a woman along beat dumping her and facing the risk of her wrath. For every guy who came clean and asked out of a relationship, there was a woman who wasn't trying to hear it and who decided to strike back. And after she's done battle with his tires, his clothes and even his house, she was satisfied. The damage she had to face had been returned, her wrath was complete and she could "exhale."

But I wasn't interested in exhaling.

I wanted to know if Eve and I had a chance. And I was willing to put it on the line to prove it. It didn't matter that Stuart was there and would rub it in my face forever if she turned me down. If she said she wanted to give things a try, the potential humiliation would be worth it.

"This isn't getting us anywhere," I commented.

"Where are we trying to get?" she asked, annoyed.

"To Cancun," Stuart replied, smiling.

"Look, Eve," I interrupted. "I'm trying to say that I care about you," I confessed. "I know we could have something special if you just gave it a try," I told her. "And I'm willing to put everything aside and give this all I can if you're even a little interested," I concluded.

"And what is it that you want, Stuart?" she asked, turning toward him.

"All I want is a date to Cancun," he answered, smiling. "All that pinning you down stuff—that's him," he said, pointing in my direction.

"You guys are too much," she said, shaking her head. "Simon," she continued softly. "You are such a wonderful man," she told me. "And you truly bring out something very special in me," she admitted. "I never knew you felt this way, but I guess I didn't want to know," she finished. "It would have stressed me out."

"I tried to tell you when we went to Nation's that night," I told her.

"She was the one who took you to Nation's?" Stuart asked, surprised.

"Don't act so surprised, Stuart," she quickly told him. "I was out with *him* while *you* were blowing up my answering machine."

"You kept me waiting for *him?*" he asked, pointing to me.

"What's that supposed to mean?" I shot back.

"Wait a minute, this isn't getting us anywhere," Eve interrupted. "Stuart, you're a nice guy, but you're naughty and I like that," she started. "I'm taken with your charm and your sense of style," she added. "And Simon, you're just a sweetheart. You're dependable, you're sensitive and you're a complete gentleman," she told me. "If I could package you two together, we'd have something *very* special," she laughed.

We just looked at her.

"Okay, bad example," she admitted. "But what can I say," she went on. "I like different things about both of you."

"I don't care about that," I insisted. "The only thing I'm interested in is making something happen with you, Eve," I added. "I'm putting it on the line like you said," I finished. "I'll commit to making it work if you will."

This was a moment men dread. Men have an unwritten

policy that says simply: Never ask a woman for a relationship until and unless you're 100 percent certain of her response. Ninety-nine percent of the time you didn't have to ask. If you'd hung around long enough, the woman assumed you were in a relationship and everything moved forward. She left a toothbrush at your place, found a way to get a copy of your keys and before you knew it, your place looked like an ad for Laura Ashley.

But that 1 percent of the time is what spooked you. You and your lady friend got along well enough. The sex was decent enough. And she didn't bother you about your whereabouts when you were out of her presence. All of which made her good wife material in your eyes. But something was missing. She still took calls in the other room, and when you were on the line with her, that annoying call-waiting buzz was a frequent visitor until well after midnight. You sensed that some other guy was involved and that the only way to push him aside was to make a real commitment and secure one from her. So even though you weren't certain she'd come your way, you broke the rule and asked, just like I'd just done. But I had to. She needed to know how I felt and that I was ready to make a move.

"Simon," she said, smiling. "I would be honored . . ."

"You would?" Stuart asked, shocked.

"I would."

"You would?" I asked, even more shocked than Stuart.

"I would," she sighed. "But this is so sudden and I have to think it through," she told me. "I have to be honest," she said, sounding worried. "This is a tough call."

"So you'll just have to choose," Stuart stated confidently.

"Yeah," I said, concerned. "But when?"

"Tomorrow," she answered, looking at her watch. "Oh my God," she said, starting to stand. "I have a one o'clock," she remarked. "I'll call you guys later and we'll talk," she added, standing between us and kissing both of us on the cheek.

I felt an incredible sense of disappointment all at once. Putting it all on the line hadn't given me the results I wanted. But if I hadn't taken the chance, the whole thing would have gotten even stickier. I couldn't imagine what Stuart was thinking, but he seemed so sure of himself, *I* was almost convinced she'd choose him. I doubted that the average guy would wait a hot minute for her to decide anything. And I knew Rod and Trevor would smack us silly for giving her the upper hand in deciding on our fates, when we both could have told her to kiss off. But I knew better. And I knew her. She was worth the wait. And I was glad I took the risk and put the ball in her court. I just hoped she bounced it the right way.

And that we'd be together when she was done.

The 60-Day Rule

Weeks 7-8

The Dawn of Destruction

I'm a numbers guy, and this thing with women—it's all in the numbers. Think about it. If I'm done with a woman in 60 days, it means that I'll date 6 women a year. Translated, I'll spend time with 12 bouncing breasts, 12 luscious legs, an untold myriad of hairstyles, 6 tight bellies, 60 elegantly manicured fingernails, 6 beautifully sculpted behinds, and 6 uniquely located G spots in any given year. Why else would I make short work of my so-called "relationships?" When I break up with a woman within 60 days, I don't have to deal with returning keys, deciding on who gets to keep any "friends" we may have made, or setting up visitation for any pets we may have purchased. I don't have to kiss the behind of parents, bosses, and roommates, because in 60 days or less chances are you'll never meet anyone significant in the woman's life. Plus, I rarely have to worry about gifts because only a true gold digger would expect anything within the first 60 days. The moment I meet a woman, I pull out my Palm Pilot and calculate when we'll enter our Dawn of Destruction. And if I handle things right, she may even like me when it's done. Which means she might get another 60 days . . . next year!

Stuart A. Worthington
The Single Stockbroker

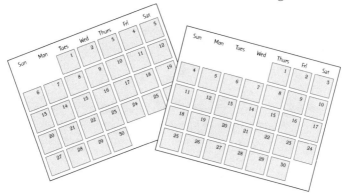

chapter 20

Lynn/Eve/Kit Kat Makes a Choice

The Next Morning

Stuart

Sleeping last night was impossible. How are you supposed to sleep when you know the woman you were
going out with has also been going out with your
friend? I didn't want Lynn like Simon did, but I wanted to
make the call on which way we were going. Who knows
what could have happened? We could have made the trip,
found we were crazy about each other and run off to Vegas
to make it official. Or maybe we would have found that all
we had in common was a love of numbers and good sex. I
wanted to find out where we really stood, and if Simon

hadn't been so busy playing Mr. Nice Guy, she'd be some-where buying clothes for Cancun right now.

I couldn't help but call Trevor and Rod to let them in on the news. They howled up a storm. And because it was a Saturday, Rod insisted we meet at my place for breakfast to hash things out. Sitting and waiting for Simon hadn't been the easiest thing in the world, but I was actually glad we were hooking up.

"What's up, fellas?" Rod asked, slowly walking in.

"How goes it, big guy?" Trevor asked.

"The gang's all here," Simon remarked, joining us.

"You two have really outdone yourselves," Trevor com-mented, shaking his head. "There are literally millions of women floating around the D.C. metropolitan area, but you guys have to go after the same one?"

"I never said I wanted her," I jumped in. "I'm just try-ing to book her for the trip."

"Why do you have to have *her* for the trip?" Rod asked. "Can't you just find somebody else?"

"Yeah," I answered, smiling. "I've already put in a call to Amber and Sonya."

"I bet they turned you down too," Simon joked.

"At least I didn't beg them to get with me," I fired back. "You guys should have heard him," I went on. " 'If you are even slightly interested, I'll give it my all,' " I said, im-itating Simon.

"You went *there*, Simon?" asked Rod.

"Why would you do that without knowing she would say yes?" Trevor added. "You know that's against the rules!"

"Because the only way I was going to get anywhere was

to take a chance," Simon explained. "When she comes back and says she's ready to get with me, you'll see what I'm talking about."

"And what if she doesn't?" Rod asked, concerned. "Have you given that any thought?"

"I may not be a marine, Rod," he answered, smiling. "But I know a thing or two about being prepared," he said, pulling out a sheet of paper. "I've got Amber and Sonya's numbers right here."

"Not an option," Trevor jumped in, shaking his head. "In fact, I'll call my friend at the Mexican consulate's office to make sure they're banned from the country that week."

"You won't have to," Simon replied. "Because Eve is going with me, so I won't need either one of them."

"So where does that leave me?" I asked.

"I may be heavy," Simon answered, starting to laugh. "But I'm not your brother," he added. "You'll have to find your own date, money."

"Trevor," Rod said, turning toward him. "What about Leigh?"

"What about her?"

"Is it too late for her to hook these fools up?" Rod asked.

"The trip is in two weeks," Trevor started. "And any woman who would be available that quick would probably be trouble," he reasoned. "Simon and Stuart," he added. "Amber and Sonya's stock just rose considerably. You may have to make that call."

"That's not happening," I said, smiling. "Simon might need to call them, but you might as well issue Lynn's ticket right now."

"My money says she'll turn both of you clowns down," Rod joked. "And I'll put a grand up that says Amber and Sonya will send you walking too."

"Wait a minute," I interrupted. "A few days ago you damn near had us digging a grave and hiring a hearse, Rod," I observed. "But now you're in full clown mode," I added. "Did you take some kind of super recovery pill or something?"

"I'll take credit where credit is due," Trevor said, starting to stand. "I got in touch with Grace, she dragged the big fella down to my office," he continued, "and let's just say we're taking a different approach to the problem."

"So what's the deal?" Simon asked. "Is he going to be okay?"

"Are you familiar with male pattern baldness?" Trevor commented.

"What did you do?" I asked, unimpressed. "Cure his cancer with Rogaine?"

"That's almost as funny as you and Simon being stuck on the same woman and not knowing it," Trevor shot back. "But Rod suffers from male pattern fear of health care," he remarked. "You tell a woman she has a yeast infection and you tell her in rare, untreated cases, the situation could be fatal and what does she do?" he asked, rhetorically. "She gets treatment, addresses the problem and then she moves on," he concluded.

"So you're treating him with Monistat, huh?" I said sarcastically.

"Not quite, but when he heard 'cancer,' he freaked," he explained. "I believe we'll get him back to where he wants to be," Trevor bragged. "And we've already discussed it, so he knows there are no guarantees."

"Yeah," Rod laughed. "Except the guarantee that says neither one of these bums can hoodwink some poor woman into a free trip to Cancun."

I worried that Rod was right. We were running out of time and waiting for Lynn was making less sense by the minute. If she decided to make a move with Simon, I was screwed. And I doubted I would make the trip, because the last thing I wanted to see was Simon sporting what should have been my date. My biggest problem, though, was the fact that she might choose me. How could I show up roaming the beaches in Cancun with the woman Simon was crazy about? I knew he said he preferred for Lynn to make the call, but that just didn't seem right.

Simon and I seemed to fall on opposite sides of almost any issue that meant anything, but he was my main man, and I wouldn't hurt him for the world. Even if it mean backing off when Lynn said, "Stuart, you're the one . You've always been the one."

I couldn't let it happen. A firm commitment to the t was all I needed. Lynn choosing me would make per sense. I knew that she couldn't do better. But that woul more harm than good at this point. Simon and I all ourselves to get caught up in some useless macho t war that ultimately would mean little. If either of the victory would be entirely empty.

Lynn was quite a prize. She was as real as rea nes. But even on her best day, she wasn't worth risk and damage she could cause to a friendship I'd f all my life. Simon was my buddy and I knew he'd alwa e there. I would have loved to run around Cancun wi the likes of Lynn in one of Cyber-Tyra's animal-print ongs, but the reality was as simple as it was complex friendship had to count for something. And Simon deserved to know it.

"Hey, Simon," I said, considering what to say.

"What's up?" he asked.

"What if I told you—" I started.

Thankfully, the doorbell was ringing, which gave me at least a minute to stall and work up a good approach. I was just glad it wasn't the phone with Lynn on the other line. She'd probably have given me the nod and then I'd have had a dilemma the size of Texas on my hands. As long as I backed out before she chose me, and I could convince Simon it was *my* choice, everything would be just fine.

"Hold that thought," I told him. "Let me get that."

I hurried to the door and was happy to find a surprisingly attractive FedEx delivery woman. She handed me a brightly colored red, white and blue envelope, and then asked for my signature.

"You can sign on the top line," she pointed out.

"You got it," I said, scribbling my name. "I must be your first delivery of the day."

"That you are," she answered. "So it's probably good [ne]ws."

"Excuse me?" I asked.

"[I] have this theory," she explained. "My first package be a good news package and then I know I'm off to a day."

"e that theory," I told her. "And I have a little theory n lf."

"Li[k] [w]hat?" she asked, smiling.

"Like en a woman with a smile as beautiful as yours is standin[g] on your porch, you invite her in," I remarked.

Van Whitfield

"Except when that woman's day just started and she has a truckload of good news to deliver around the city," she shot back.

"Point well taken," I replied, now smiling like I'd hit the lottery. "But you can't be working forever."

"Agreed," she answered, tearing off a piece of paper. "Here's my number," she said, writing on a notepad. "Call me sometime and we'll chat."

"Why don't you take my number too?" I asked, reaching for her pen.

"I already have it," she replied, displaying a copy of the air-bill and walking toward her truck.

"Charmaine!" I exclaimed, reading from the sheet with her number.

"Yes, Mr. Worthington!" she answered, reading from the air-bill and then jumping in the truck.

"Have you ever been to Cancun on New Year's Eve?!"

"Not yet, but send me a ticket and I'll meet you there!" she yelled, pulling away.

Charmaine, I thought, turning to walk back inside. *I don't know what her plans are for this evening, but they just changed.*

"Who was that this early in the morning?" Rod asked, peeling an orange.

"It was just the FedEx lady," I answered, placing the package on an ottoman.

"The FedEx *lady*," Trevor asked. "I'm surprised you didn't ask *her* to go on the trip."

"He probably did," Simon joked.

"How did you know?" I asked, surprised.

"Have you lost your mind, Stu," Rod asked, standing up.

"How can the biggest player in D.C. be so incredibly desperate?" Trevor wondered. "Why don't you drive down to that Amoco on the corner and ask the attendant if she'd like to go?"

"She's married," I answered.

"You're pathetic," Simon reasoned.

"Whatever happened to your policy on blue collar women, Stuart?" Trevor asked. "I thought you didn't date them."

"I don't and I never will," I told him. "I was going to set them up with Simon," he said, laughing.

"Hey," Rod said, dropping a peel into a trash can. "Does your office ever give you a break? Why are they sending you a FedEx on a Saturday?"

"Who knows?" I answered, walking into the kitchen. "Maybe some client is sending me a tip for making him rich."

"Do you have a client named Evelyn Chambers?" Trevor asked, inspecting the envelope.

"Damn," I yelled, dropping a glass. "She sent something here?"

"You live here, don't you?" Simon asked, now holding the envelope. "Where else would she send it?"

"To your place," Trevor laughed.

"She knows you guys swing together," Rod added, laughing.

"I liked you a lot better when you were dying from cancer last week," Simon fired back. "What do we have to do to get the kinder, gentler Rod back?"

"You have to open that envelope and see what creative measures she used to dump you clowns," Rod told him, laughing.

I didn't want to do that. Charmaine, who was now easily my favorite FedEx employee, predicted it would be good news. Which actually, at this point, would be bad news. I couldn't afford for Lynn to say yes. That just couldn't happen. But it was in the cards. I always knew she'd pick me, it was the only move that made sense. Even as she kissed us both on the cheek when she left yesterday, the kiss she gave me *had* to mean much more to her. But what could I do? The fellas were all here and I was going to be forced to read it out loud and break Simon's heart.

But not before I backed out and give him a chance to save face.

"Simon," I said, turning toward him. "I need to say something."

"The hell you do," Rod jumped in. "You already know that she picked him so you're going to try to back out and let yourself off the hook."

"Can it, Rod," I answered. "I already know she picked me."

"And how might you know that?" Trevor asked, handing the envelope to Rod.

"Because Charmaine told me it was good news," I admitted.

"Charmaine?" Simon asked, surprised. "Who the hell is Charmaine?"

"She's the FedEx lady," I responded.

"You know her name?" Trevor asked, worried.

"Do I know her name?" I scoffed. "I have her number. I got it for Simon, because he's going to need it."

"That does it," Rod said, ripping the envelope open. "We need to read this thing right now, so we'll have enough time to get this fool to a shrink."

I immediately thought of how I'd react. She was choosing me and I was certain even Simon knew it. I tried to back out, but not in the way Rod portrayed it. I wanted to make sure Simon had what he wanted. He wanted a real shot with Lynn. He felt they had a connection and that they could make a real go of it. Knowing how Lynn felt about me, I doubt that Simon would get far with her. But he wanted that chance and I wanted to ensure it for him. And after Rod read her note, and she'd agreed to swing with me, Simon would be crushed.

Rod carefully pulled a tiny white notecard-size envelope from the FedEx pack, and slowly started to read it.

"Dear Stuart," he started. "My choice has been made. Please know that I've sent this to Simon as well."

This was going to be tough. I didn't want to gloat. That wouldn't be right. I just didn't want Simon to be humiliated in front of the group.

"Here goes," Rod said, pulling out another cream-colored, textured-looking card. "Ms. Evelyn Chambers and Mr. Victor A. D'mazio are pleased to announce the occasion of their wedding on January 1, 2001."

"What?!" I exclaimed, shocked.

"Now that's what I call a creative measure," Rod joked. "She'd rather walk down the aisle than to get stuck with one of you losers."

"She's marrying Vic?" Simon added, surprised.

"Don't tell me you know Vic too?" Trevor asked.

"You remember Big Pussy from D & B's, Stu?" Simon remarked, looking toward me.

"She's marrying one of the Sopranos?" asked Trevor.

"You mean the old Italian guy you got jammed with in the bathroom?" I remarked, stunned.

"You got it," Simon answered, in a haze.

"You got caught with one of the Sopranos in a bathroom?" Trevor asked, concerned. "Did you at least get his autograph on some toilet paper?"

"Site and time to be determined," Rod read on, laughing. "Hope y'all can make it!" he said, laughing even more.

I couldn't believe it. What in the world was Lynn thinking? She was marrying a guy who might be old enough to be her father's father. How could she do this? I was certain she would pick me. I was so worried about Simon, I hadn't considered there could be someone else.

"She wrote something on the back too," Rod told us, flipping the card. "Dear Stuart," he read. "I know this seems sudden, and I do apologize, but yesterday put everything into perspective," he added. "Simon followed his heart, which helped me to realize I needed to do the same," he went on. "It was the last minute and we wanted to get the word out, so we had some quickie invites done yesterday. I'm sure we'll do something formal too, but that's beside the point. I wanted you and Simon to be the first to know, because I didn't want to hold up your trip," he recited. "Both of you are very special men who will make someone very happy," he said, finishing. "Enjoy Cancun and happy holidays."

"Happy holidays?" I asked, feeling crushed. "There's no way we can have a happy holiday," I reasoned.

"Yeah there is," Simon remarked, reaching in his pocket. "I've got the answer right here," he added, reaching for the phone.

"What are you doing, Simon?" Trevor asked, cleaning his glasses.

"He's probably calling Eve to see if he can come to the wedding," Rod joked.

"Hello," Simon started, speaking into the receiver. "Yes," he added, his head nodding. "I'm trying to reach Amber and Sonya," he continued. "Oh," he said, sounding surprised. "I didn't know," he went on. "No," he finished. "No message."

"You really called them?" I asked, worried.

"You know I did," he responded.

"So what happened?" Rod asked, smiling.

"They got married," Simon told us, shaking his head.

"To who?" I said, jumping in. "The mayor of their trailer park?!"

"Somebody in here owes me a grand!" Rod happily exclaimed.

"Lighten up, big fella," begged Trevor. "This is no easy loss," he stressed. "The trip is right around the corner," he added. "What do you think they can do?"

I knew just what I would do. And just like Simon did for Lynn, she edged me toward a decision. I wanted to go to Cancun, have a ball and wipe out all of this craziness. There was only one way to do it and it was about to get done.

I was going to follow my heart.

And my phone was going to get me there.

"Hello, this is Stuart Worthington," I said, stepping into the next room. "And we met when you dropped a package at my place this morning," I said, after her answering machine picked up. "Your theory about good news in your first delivery didn't work out, so I can only hope the rest of your day went okay," I started. "Look, Charmaine, I know

this is coming out of the blue, and I swear I'm not a nut,"
I added. "But remember when I asked you about Cancun
on New Year's Eve and you said to send you a ticket?" I
asked, concerned. "Well, I was just wondering," I finished.
"Where should I send the ticket?"

There. It was done. My date was all but set. Who needed
a flake like Lynn/Eve/Kit Kat? Cancun at New Year's
would be right. Even if we couldn't drink the fricking
water. I couldn't wait. We'd probably made way too much
of this trip, but after Amber and Sonya last year, anybody
would. We had a chance to reconnect and rewrite the woes
of last year's trip, which had gone woefully wrong. I was
set. But what was Simon going to do? There was no way he
was going to dig up somebody in a week.

Or so I thought.

"Hey, Stu!" he yelled, before I hung up. "See if she has
a sister for me!"

June 2001

Simon

Things have a funny way of working themselves out. Finding that Eve and Lynn were one in the same was tough. I always believed that women didn't know what they wanted, but she proved me wrong. It's easy to say women don't know what they want, especially when what they don't want is *you*. Eve knew exactly what she wanted, which is why she married the veritable king of D.C.'s gentlemen's clubs, Vic. I'd be lying if I said it didn't throw me for a total loop. I was crushed. Make that *beyond* crushed. But I'm a guy, so saying, "I was crushed," sounds cleaner than admitting, "She hurt me." It may sound different, but, eerily, it feels the same.

It took me hitting the big 3-0 to make me finally take a chance and put my feelings on the line. And what did I end up with? A cheesy two-buck wedding announcement from the woman *I was* supposed to be with. I still don't know how I got so hung up on a woman who was so clearly unavailable, but they say the woman who takes your virginity can have that effect on you.

I felt like a fool for putting myself out there, but if I had to, I'd do it all over again. I still think Eve was worth it. And her words still ring in my ears: "... if you're not willing to take the risk of getting hurt to get what you really want, you're a chump." I may have lost out on her, but one thing's for certain, I'm nobody's chump. The minidepression I survived proved that. I didn't answer the phone for a week, called in sick to work and couldn't eat, which was actually a good thing.

I joined Weight Watchers and started an exercise program, which helped me make a dramatic change—I've lost twenty pounds!

Trevor, Leigh and little Trevor still look like they were plucked from a Norman Rockwell painting. I've never known people who so readily accepted their family roles. Trevor's still a snob, Leigh's still a living, breathing trophy and little Trevor is a ten-year-old earring-wearing brat.

Rod and Grace are as happy as ever. Thanks to Trevor, Rod confronted his prostate cancer head-on. And much like New York's ghoulish mayor, Rudy Giuliani, he beat it. The twins, Koko and Loko, graduate this month and they've both been accepted to Wellesley College, the ritzy, very private *all-girls* school in New England. Rod is still the heart and soul of our group and because of him and the troubles he faced, we've all committed to an annual check-up and promised to request those annoying prostate exams.

Stuart is still a nut.

The man who never met a relationship he liked *or* a woman who could "slow his roll" now has his nose wide open. He and Charmaine are a full-fledged item and she's blown his 60-day rule to bits. No one can believe that Stuart Alexander Worthington is head over heels in love with a *blue collar woman* who wears a uniform to work, but he is. He's also proven to be an able companion for her two kids, Daryl and Stephanie. He says they're a handful and that he nearly ended the relationship when he first met them, but he knew how much he liked Charmaine, so he gave them a chance.

She's the only woman I'm aware of who's given him a challenge. She's funny, extremely bright and as honest as a monk. On their first real date, Stuart arrived at her door dressed to the nines. When he proudly asked, "So how do I look?" she laughed and said, "You didn't tell me we were going to a meeting, I thought we were going on a date." That was four months ago and amazingly, Stuart the club rat hasn't been to a club or worn a tie since. Banded-collar shirts and silk tees now dominate his wardrobe.

Cancun was great. It easily surpassed all of our past trips. Rod's prostate problem changed his perspective about a great many things. And the day after Christmas he declared that our annual trip would be a wide open, full-blown family affair. Koko and Loko were going. Little Trevor would be there. And with three days to go, Stuart and I *still* didn't have dates. True to his word, he asked Charmaine about her sister, but we didn't get past the first date. She was as cute as Charmaine. But she'd been married and divorced twice. And her three kids, by three different men, all called me "Daddy!" when I went to pick her up.

Stuart tried every trick in the book to convince Charmaine to go, but they'd just met and she wasn't having it. She was still *"kind of seeing someone,"* as she put it, so Stuart backed off. We exhausted our Rolodexes, Palm Pilots and old school little black books trying to pin down someone. But it wasn't happening.

Then one day, Stuart struck gold.

"This is going to seem far-fetched," he told me, logging on to his computer. "But I think it might work."

"Do you not remember meeting Amber and Sonya online?" I asked, concerned.

"They say lightning rarely strikes the same place twice, so we're probably safe," he joked.

He pecked away at the keyboard and moments later, turned to me smiling. "We'll have an answer in the morning," he boasted.

"An answer to what?" I asked, worried.

I shouldn't have been worried. Stuart was a master manipulator who could scheme with the best of them. And when you put someone like him up against the wall, you can count on only the best results. He rang me the next morning and said casually, "It's on, money. Santa Claus just called."

"Did you find out why he's three days late?" I said, unimpressed.

"It's our fault," he explained. "We just didn't ask for the right things."

"We didn't happen to ask for Amber and Sonya's sisters, did we?" I nervously asked.

"Simon," he said, sighing. "Have I ever let you down?"

"Where do you want me to start?" I asked, yawning.

"I'll see you in Cancun," he told me.

"And who will we see you with?" I shot back.

"Relax, Simon," he insisted. "We just hit the jackpot."

Little did I know how much of a jackpot we'd hit. Our plane got held up on the runway and we arrived in sunny Cancun nearly three hours late. During the flight I couldn't help but wonder what Stuart had done, and who we'd run from this year. I wanted to have a good time and to put Eve far out of my mind.

And when we finally made it to our compound and opened the door to our villa, my mouth slowly muttered, "Who the hell was Eve?"

Stuart had pulled off a miracle.

"Turvy!" I happily exclaimed. "Is that you?!"

"I'm Topsy," she answered, rising to reveal one of Cyber-Tyra's animal-print thongs. "Turvy's in the Jacuzzi."

The rest is history. We had the ball of balls. They lived up to their videos, their calendars and their website, where

Stuart had contacted them. He barely spoke to either of them the entire trip. His ear was glued to the phone, trying to kick things off with Charmaine. To this day, I don't know what he promised them or how much he put out. I do know that he did it to help me get over Eve. And boy did it work. The moment my foot hit the bubbly water in the Jacuzzi, she was all but forgotten.

Suffice it to say, I've already booked *both* of them for next year's trip.

And I may very well take them if things don't pan out with the woman I'm seeing these days, Patrice. Stuart assured me he'd never seen her after I introduced them, which I felt was a major plus. She's not an exotic ex-dancer like Eve. She doesn't have a website like Topsy and Turvy. And from an appearance standpoint, she's as average as they come. It's not like I lowered my standards with her. If anything, after Eve, my standards rose through the roof.

Patrice and I met entirely by accident. We were seated in a tiny, crowded waiting room, nervously flipping through magazines.

"This is your first time, isn't it?" I asked, reaching for a copy of *VIBE* magazine.

"It shows that much?" she answered, looking up.

"I wouldn't go that far," I replied. "But I remember my first time like it was yesterday."

"Was it as hard as they say it is?"

"Harder," I admitted.

"But you're still coming," she remarked. "It couldn't have been that bad."

"It was," I explained. "But if it weren't tough, it wouldn't be worth doing."

"I'll have to remember that," she told me.

"Take my number," I said, tearing away a corner of the magazine.

"Washington!" yelled a voice I'd become all too familiar with. "Get in here on the double!"

It was Mrs. Platz, and I knew exactly what that yell meant. B.L. and Marc had just arrived and she wanted them out of her office.

The moment the trip ended, I'd hurried to call Mrs. Platz. I invited Stuart in, but he wasn't having it. The debacle at D & B's had done it for him. During the trip, I watched as Rod and Trevor interacted with their kids and marveled at the love, guidance and reassurance they so easily provided. It made me think of Eve, who one day was choosing between me and Stuart, and the next, was shopping for a wedding ring. I recalled how feeling so thoroughly disposable was the worst thing I'd ever experienced. And I knew Stuart and I had done the same exact thing to Marc and B.L.

I hated myself for it and knew I'd never again allow them to feel like I had.

I've seen them every single week since I've been back from Cancun and my life is better for it. I've already enrolled them in camp for the summer, made them get library cards and have seen their grades rise at a steady, satisfying pace. It's amazing what a dose of discipline, concern and understanding can do for a child. I've learned to take the bad with the good and now better understand the intricacies of games like tee-ball and soccer, both of which they play. They even helped me to fulfill my lifelong dream, which Eve had once squashed.

I called a scalper friend of mine who rounded up three tickets and Marc, B.L. and I flew to Tampa to see my beloved Colts claim the Vince Lombardi trophy for Maryland.

We went to the Super Bowl!

We were walking around the Air and Space Museum last month and I delighted in their amazement at the planes, models and exhibits that abound in the huge halls. Suddenly, I knew what I had to do. I called my attorney, and had him call Mrs. Platz and jumped in all the way. If things go as they should, the adoption should clear sometime next year. In the meantime, they'll stay with me for the summer so we can see if we're a real fit.

Stuart says I'm crazy and Rod and Trevor think I've lost my mind.

Maybe they're right.

But when I walk through the door and their eyes light up like Christmas trees, I know I've made the right decision. And because there's a God, the likelihood of us becoming a real family grows stronger as each day passes. In a wonderfully satisfying way, the kids and I need each other. And the security they've found from knowing I'm a permanent fixture in their lives has given them the one thing they've never truly known.

Peace.

After the debacle with Eve, Stuart said I should write a book. I didn't think I'd take it that far, but I followed his suggestion and purchased a journal. I sat down in front of my fireplace one night and curled up with a six-pack of Bud and my journal. I couldn't help but smile as I watched Eve's once dreaded "It's over" note go up in flames. It was exactly the type of closure I needed. I've learned some valuable lessons in the last year, but what sticks out the most is something I wrote one night last week:

We stretched out on the grounds of the Washington Monument, and lying on our backs, gazed at the beautiful, star-filled, evening sky. B.L. lay to my left side and Marc was on my right.

"Look at the stars, find one you like and reach out for it," I told them. "If you want to make something of your life, you can't be afraid to reach for the stars."

After just a few minutes of reaching in vain they were ready to give up.

"It'd be cool to have a star," Marc remarked, still looking up. "But what am I going to do with it anyway?"

"Yeah," B.L. agreed, his hands still outstretched. "I want one, but it's not like I have to have it," he reasoned. "But if I did need one," he explained. "My arms would stay up there until one came down to me."

It hit me.

Our arms will reach only so far for the things we think we want. But it's amazing how hard we'll fight for the things we really need.

Life *does* go on even after you've been crushed.

I know.

Mine did.

Incredible.